FRACTURED SOLITUDE

LET THOSE SPARKLES OF HOPE KEEP SHINING EVEN WHEN LIFE SEEMS DARK. WE ARE NEVER TRULY ALONE.

BADAL VERMA

INDIA • SINGAPORE • MALAYSIA

ISBN
Paperback 979-8-89699-510-4
Hardcase 979-8-89699-909-6

Disclaimer

This is a work of fiction. All characters in this book are fictional and imaginary. Any similarity with any person, living or dead, is purely coincidental.

For Varsha

To love life, to love even when you have no stomach for it and everything you've held dear crumbles like burnt paper in your hands, your throat filled with the silt of it. When grief sits with you, it's tropical heat thickening the air, heavy as water more fit for gills than lungs; when grief weights you like your own flesh, only more of it, an obesity of grief, you think, how can a body withstand this? Then you hold the life like a face between your palms, a plain face, no charming smile, no violet eyes, and you say, yes, I will take you; I will make you smile again; I will love you, again, and dance freely, with the wounds beneath my feet …

Contents

ACKNOWLEDGEMENTS

When I first sit down to write a book, the creation begins as a joyful yet solitary one; there is just the Universe and me. Then, gradually, the circle begins to widen because every accomplishment requires the efforts of many people and this book is no different. Thank you, thank you, thank you: my wife Varsha whose belief in me inspired, guided, encouraged, and nudged me to start writing and helped me write every day. One fine day she decided to proceed to her heavenly abode and I was left alone by the divine dictate. That separation and her love formed the basis of Fractured Solitude. In that sense, this book is more hers than mine.

Thank you to my daughter Neetisha for her probing questions, subtle hints, and useful inputs which made me a better writer.

Many examples, stories, and anecdotes are the result of a collection from various sources, such as newspapers, social media, other speakers, seminar participants, and more importantly the waves of the wisdom of the indigenous people and ingenious practices I inherited in the travails trailing my travels over the past 57 years that helped me write this book. Unfortunately, sources were not always noted or available; hence, it became impractical to provide an accurate acknowledgement. Regardless of the source, I wish to express my gratitude to those who may have contributed to this book, even though anonymously. However, every effort has been made to give credit, where it is due, for the material contained herein. Thank you all very much.

And above all, thank you: to myself, who suffered so many moods and emotional mayhem over the course of creating this book, and tempered and tolerated the many bouts of both megalomania and utter despair that came with writing it. What an absolute privilege to have me as a first reader and editor and the most perfect companion of my solitude. How did I get so lucky to have tricked myself into being in me? I love every single thing about you. Thank you most of all.

Foreword

"I am glad the rain is coming down hard. It's the way I feel inside."

Fractured Solitude is a tale of an Army veteran, a young entrepreneur, and a homemaker, who are brought together by a twist of fate.... unaware companions on the ship of life sailing through the ocean of grief.

The book took me back to the autumn of 2021, which is when I lost a piece of my heart forever. I haven't been the same since then or so I am told. I am unable to recall what I was like before it all happened. The woman in my iPhone photo gallery appears to be a doppelgänger of the woman standing before the mirror. But there are differences that I can see...the woman in the photo gallery has radiance on her skin, a twinkle of hope in her eyes, and anticipation of life in her smile. Where did all that vanish? Did it vanish? Or is it shrouded in a cloud of grief?

Is grief really a cloud? After all, it has been three years now. Aren't clouds supposed to clear at some point in time? What about the accompanying loneliness and depression? Can one wish them away...pray them away...medicate them away or meditate them away? Honestly, I have tried everything but they still seem to be there…they now live in me.

Deep in my thoughts, I involuntarily start humming the 'Numb Little Bug' by Em Beihold… *"Do you ever get a little bit tired of life…*

Like you're not really happy but you don't wanna die, like you're hanging by a thread but you gotta survive, 'Cause you gotta survive, like your body's in the room but you're not really there, like you have empathy inside but you don't really care, like you're fresh outta love but it's been in the air…Am I past repair??"

I guess I have made my peace with my loneliness and depression and perhaps acceptance is the key…. maybe I am in fact the numb little bug that's gotta survive!

Would I ever be the same again? Would I ever feel whole again? These are questions I don't have an answer to but perhaps that feeling of nothingness and the void in the heart are my ode to the love I harbour for my mother.

Reading through Fractured Solitude, I couldn't help but wonder if I identified more with Nuvem or Shibra or Zainab, or all of them. It made me wonder if the grieving self, at whatever stage it might be, finds resonance with another grieving soul. And most importantly, is there hope after all that the nimbus cloud of SMOTH will give way to sunshine?

I hope this book does the same for you as it did for me – a trip down memory lane, a sneak peek into the locked corner of my heart, and a tiny ray of hope that someday I would also learn to dance with wounds beneath my feet.

- Neetisha Verma

Author's Note

"It's your road and yours alone. Others may walk it with you, but no one can walk it for you. But don't feel alone, there's always someone who silently cares for you."

Loneliness is solitary and it is universal at the same time. But we are never truly alone. There is someone who silently takes care. Loneliness is perplexing and painful, but essentially it is only an illusion, a mask created by the surface consciousness. Losing a soulmate compels one to bear the unbearable and the protagonist goes through a hell of pain and suffering after losing the woman he loved the most and who loved him even more.

The Fractured Solitude traces his journey of hope from utter depression to the pressing compulsion and deep desire to heal and accept being a new him. Life reveals to him that if he is lonely, he stands on a bridge between two worlds: one of lack and the other of plentitude. The lack creates a vacuum that can only be assuaged if he adopts a conscious approach. He has to accept he cannot simply stand and stare at his wounds forever. He knows and believes that the only antidote to mental agony is physical pain. His soldierly instincts prompt him to step out of his comfort zone and travel extensively with a firm belief that everything happens for a reason; every single thing, the good and bad all will lead him to where he is meant to be. As he ventures far and wide into the difficult areas, the serendipity of travelling and conscious breathing blesses him. The physics of his quest takes him to the places where he discovers a fresh paradigm and suddenly his pain appears tiny in comparison to the scale of the natural upheaval of the universe. In such wonderful places, he experiences a feeling akin to Nirvana and thereafter he learns to smile even with moist eyes.

He embraces the privileges of solitude and accepts the possibility that life may break to be more beautiful. He learns that solitude is a discipline, a norm that empowers his aloneness. Aloneness is a happy state of loneliness and a practical state of solitude and in that sense, aloneness is The Fractured Solitude. Solitude is destined to be fractured by the memories of his wife which ironically sings the song of love as well. He battles the hypocrisy of being human; the constant tug between solitude and company, the desire to love so desperately and simultaneously be detached from it all, of wanting everything or wanting nothing. Paradoxically, he also learns that the ability to be alone is also the condition for the ability to love. In his journey of recovery, he meets two women who authenticate his desire and need to let go and lighten up.

In the end, he makes peace and positions himself to pursue happiness as a military drill and discipline. And slowly, he accesses the art of dancing freely with wounds beneath his feet.

In the end, he chooses himself, and the story begins …

- Badal Verma

SHE MUST LIVE

"I am a self-destructive storm. A tempest within echoes unrest, thunder rumbles, mayhem in the head, thoughts unclear, and emotions manifest. I am a self-destructive storm. Relentless to see the skies clearing, the lightcning of doubt strikes at the heart, and tears precipitate as rainfall. I am a self-destructive storm."

– WhatVasThinks

Nuvem was in a state of happiness. The party with National Defence Academy (NDA) coursemates had just finished and he was reasonably high on old memories and some Pisco Porton, a Producto De Peru. Everyone wanted him to stay, but he was keen to return to his home away from home at Fagu. It was past midnight, quite cold, and a drizzle signalled an impending snowfall at Narkanda. Perhaps Nuvem Verma was missing someone even in one of the most lively and likable company of friends and their spouses.

He came out and literally jogged to escape the cold raindrops to the black beauty, his Creta Sx Executive. As soon as he pushed the ignition, he felt Vrishti come, sit next to him, and lovingly admonished, "Let me drive you drunkard." Vrishti was a better driver though she learnt to drive much later in life than him and she always drove him home safely when he was high on happiness.

That thought brought tears to his eyes as usual. Those divine drops in his eyes for the initial thirty minutes of his journey by now are a mandatory ritual, a Shubh Mahurat, a good omen, which he believes makes his solo travels safer and more mindful. Only memories that catalyse such precious emotions will differ every time for a similar outcome.

He wanted her to drive, but Vrishti was only a beautiful feeling, a sacred memory. He smiled and said, "You know I drive better when I am a bit high," and pressed the throttle.

The weather was turning hostile and choosing to drive the 40 km stretch over the winding mountainous road from Narkanda to Fagu was not a good idea. Nuvem was in a hard-earned contentment and enjoyment phase of his fractured life, dwelling in a space that was out beyond the idea of being good or bad, wrong or right.

Not that he wasn't adoringly admonished by those who loved and cared for him, but he normally stopped listening to anyone, including himself at times in utter recklessness, total Awargi. That was the new normal in his life. He roamed about carrying a lot of love stored within but …

He was quite familiar with hill driving and had driven on Narkanda-Fagu road twice in the recent past. The night driving in the mountains was always easier than the day driving because the headlights gave an early indication of the vehicles approaching from the opposite direction. Another advantage accrued in the night was that the perpetually erring local taxi drivers kept to their side on the road bends.

Perhaps, owing to the inclement weather and unearthly hours, vehicles were far and few that night. As he took control of his driving anxieties and instincts, Nuvem remembered Taylor Swift's song "Lover" was played over and over again at their party earlier in the night. A spontaneous smile broke out on his face and he asked Alexa to play "Lover" on Amazon music yet again.

For whatever reason Nuvem loved every time she repeated and reemphasised "Lover" in the song. For some reason or logic of his guilt, he was fixated on 'Lover', especially the way it was said in the song with a cocktail of the embedded emotions of sadness and sarcasm, jealousy, or maybe anger, or maybe love.

He experienced Taylor Swift's 'Lover' emoting the scenario of his inner realm. He smiled at the ability of men to connect anything to everything when it came to women. Nuvem was nefariously naughty at times. Fortunately, he never considered that fun fullness as an escape mechanism. For it was like he had learnt to dance freely with the wound beneath his feet! And, in doing so, he took care not to hurt the sentiments of anybody.

He remembered asking two pretty Mizo girls to sing that song at Hotel Holiday Inn, Jaipur one night. And for whatever reason, the girls giggled and said, "We knew this coming from you." There was no need to know what those girls meant by what they said because Nuvem knew exactly why he requested them to sing that particular song. It reminded him that he didn't love her enough. The song is not a song until it is sung!!!

He, for sure, was not a "Swiftie" though he was mighty impressed by her aura and era, and "Swiftonomics."

While coming down the slope on the winding road, Nuvem observed headlights, perhaps on the high beam from a distance. As he came closer, he realised that those headlights were stationary and even the blinkers were on. Fearing some sort of unknown trouble, he switched off the music and drove cautiously while drawing nearer to the stationary vehicle.

The vehicle was on the road bend, its headlights blinded him and he couldn't make out what that vehicle was. As he passed that vehicle, the headlights of his Creta shone on a lanky silhouette of a woman on a road protection concrete barrier teetering on the edge of the deep valley surely contemplating suicide or so he thought.

Nuvem was shaken to the core by the dangerous sight that suddenly presented itself to his view on a lonely spot. He instinctively applied brakes as Creta came to a screeching halt by the side of the road.

Nuvem Verma was an Infantry Veteran and surely, he had seen more ghastly and grossly intimidating sights in his active service than the one he was seeing now. But that was a new view and at 68, he was vastly shaken by the prospects of witnessing the possible loss of a young life in such a cowardly manner.

He came out of the car and stood still. That's what made sense to him because he didn't know what to do and any proactive move by him could hasten the loss of that precious life. He had recently overcome a state of deep depression owing to the loss of a beautiful woman whom he loved and for that reason, he could relate to the emotional mayhem the young woman could be experiencing in those extremely distressing moments of hers.

He kept quiet, didn't try to reason with her, simply waited, watched, and hoped for some miracle to unfold and save her life. She was soaked in rain and shivering in the cold. Nuvem's heart jumped in his throat as she inched forward and stood on her heels on the road barrier while her feet were hanging in the valley. She was shivering, swaying, and shaking, but not falling.

That was a positive sign for it indicated her unwillingness to end her life yet. This thought was drawn from a memory of himself standing similarly on the edge of the seven-metre platform and not jumping while everyone coaxed him to jump, pass the swimming test, and save his relegation at the National Defence Academy, Khadakwasla, Pune.

He remembered standing on his heels many times on that seven-metre-high platform but never jumped on his own. He was pushed and thrown into the pool several times before he overcame the fear of the unknown and jumped on his own. So, he hoped she should live.

In the given situation, her circumstances could be exhorting her to take the plunge, but she was afraid of jumping to her possible death. Whether that logic made sense or not, it gave him hope that she wouldn't jump. She quietly stepped down. The Life triumphed and Nuvem was hugely relieved in a eureka moment of shared humanity. He ran forward and hugged her tightly while tears swelled in his eyes. She was cold, her eyes were blank, and she stood in his arms nonchalantly, as if she had given up on living while being alive. Sadness is indeed dark, deep, and depressing.

Suddenly the sky lit up in a rumble of thunder as the snowflakes started falling. Nuvem hurried her into his car and covered her in a blanket. He switched off the headlights and ignition of her black Mercedes and locked the car.

When he came back to his car, she was sleeping peacefully. He drove her to Fagu. He had come to Fagu searching for an idea in solitude for his next book and was staying in the beautiful and luxurious outhouse of his friends Bhasins, the renowned businessmen, based at Ludhiana.

Before starting from there, Nuvem had called Keenie, the caretaker, to keep one room ready for her as well. They reached Fagu almost at 3:00 A.M. Keenie was there to receive them and he helped him park the car in the narrow garage in the basement.

Thereafter, he fetched her bags as Nuvem escorted her to her room which was cosy and aesthetically organised. She had some hot water. He asked her not to lock her room after she changed her clothes. She gave a feeble smile and latched the door.

Nuvem gave the necessary instructions to Keenie and asked him to arrange for a local driver to get her car back to Fagu later in the day. While going past her room he looked inside briefly. She was fast asleep unmindful of what happened just a few hours ago. He smiled, closed her room, and went to sleep.

He got up at about 9:00 A.M. and again glanced into her room through the doors. She was still sleeping peacefully and her innocent face was glowing from the reflected light of the flames from the fireplace which Keenie had lit earlier in the morning.

She woke up around 11:00 A.M. By then Nuvem had finished his breakfast and he was ready in his trekking kit to move out. Nuvem greeted her warmly as she came into the living room and he introduced himself to her, "Hi, I am Lieutenant Colonel Nuvem Verma, an Indian Army Veteran."

She smiled and said, "Good Morning Sir. I am Shibra, Shibra Salim Khan," and hastened to add, "I am really hungry."

Nuvem smiled at her comfy informality and said, "Okay, so we have hot "Parathas" and omelette for breakfast or brunch whatever you may call it. Sit on the dining table and just attack."

She ate quietly, had her fill, and asked, "Are you going out trekking?"

"Yes, I am planning to just walk up to the temple on the nearby hill to compensate for the sins of the last night at Narkanda, and be guilt-free for the ones I have planned for the evening."

Shibra didn't understand much, looked quite lost, and said, "Can I come with you?"

"Sure."

"Just give me ten minutes to get ready."

Nuvem was wondering at the sheer disdain with which the young woman was treating her predawn misadventure as if what happened there was quite normal for her. She had no remorse and she was trying to be normal though her fidgety demeanour was cheating her sense of an outward composure.

Sense, Sensibility, and Sanity

"We are never really alone. Some invisible Power protects all of us all the time."

Going to Deshu Mata Temple was a ritual that Nuvem followed every time he visited Fagu. The famous Deshu Mata Temple was situated at the Fagu Top which rose as a continuation of the spur on which Bhasins' outhouse was located. It wasn't very far, just 400 steps to it from there, and it normally took about half an hour of steep climb to reach up to the temple.

During their last visit to Fagu some fifteen years ago, Vrishti and Nuvem reached the top of the hill at an altitude of more than 10826 feet above the mean sea level in just twenty minutes. They paid their obeisance to the deity and thereafter sat at a place that presented a beautiful canvas of nature to their view. That was a convenient and comfortable place to contemplate and manifest the energy and peace of the environment.

However, given his age of sixty-eight years, ongoing medication for blood pressure and diabetes, the rarity of oxygen at that elevation, and the absence of Vrishti in his lacklustre life, this time he hoped to climb up to the Deshu Mata Temple in approximately one hour.

Shibra and Nuvem stepped out of the warmth of the home and immediately encountered cold winds, it was a cold forenoon. The climb started immediately and Nuvem struggled to steady the symmetry of his steps and walked up slowly while breathing heavily. Shibra deliberately slowed down and adjusted her pace to be with him. After about ten minutes of climb, Nuvem was comfortable and they walked normally thereafter.

They generally conversed about the cold climate. Normally weather is what you talk about when you have nothing else to say. But that chat that day was necessary to break the ice between them for a larger conversation that should follow a little later and they obviously had a lot to talk about.

After some time as he got tired, Nuvem stopped speaking. Shibra understood and they measured the rest of the steps of the higher elevations quietly. Finally, they arrived at the highest point of the hill where Deshu Mata Temple was located.

Nuvem came there after over fifteen years and to his pleasant surprise the very small, unkept, and deserted temple of the deity then had been renovated into a grand temple of Deshu Mata and the temple complex was full of devotees and tourists.

Nuvem spent some forty-five minutes there and thereafter sat down to meditate at a quiet corner of the temple complex. Shibra was with him throughout and she also meditated with Nuvem. They sat into the meditative endeavour for not more than ten minutes.

Nuvem had read a lot about the powers of meditation and heard about the experiences of some saints and monks as well. But all he could reach was a level of meditative state of his mind from where he could continuously expel the waves of his thoughts as they arose. Fortunately, even that was relaxing.

On the other hand, Shibra couldn't concentrate, her mind agitated, and she spent those ten minutes waiting for Nuvem to open his eyes. Her ordeal was over when Nuvem opened his eyes after some time which for Shibra seemed like an eternity. Thereafter, she followed Nuvem who was looking for his favourite place to sit and contemplate.

The place where Nuvem sat last time, after praying at the temple, was unrecognisable. So, they climbed up a little further to sit at a convenient and quieter place to manifest in the abundance of mother nature.

Shibra gave him some hot water from her thermos and they sat quietly for a long time. Shibra keenly observed Nuvem all this while. She was in her early thirties and she was intrigued to find the striking similarities Nuvem shared with her father whom she lost some three years ago.

Shibra knew she was a difficult child, but her father loved her in every way and she was always herself when she was in his company. Whenever she messed up big time, which she often did, she would go to him but he would keep quiet and expect her to start the conversation.

Shibra was further intrigued that even when her behaviour that morning was at its nadir, Nuvem never spoke about it. Was he going to be her Blue? Her feelings hardly had any basis, they had just met a few hours ago. But then some random feelings can become the basis of enduring relationships of destiny. Not able to hold her curiosity any longer, Shibra approached him indirectly and asked, "You came all the way up here for this crowded and noisy temple?"

Nuvem looked at her vulnerable face, smiled, and said "No, I came up to absorb the energies of Deshu Mata as also those of the collective faith of the natives and sit here in the blessings of the beautiful environment of this place." And a cordial conversation crept up quietly as he quipped, "Do you have faith in someone or something?"

"No, not whatsoever, especially after my father died. I hate Allah", she was angry and blunt.

"Not even the Creator of this Universe whoever she or he is?"

"Creator in unverifiable."

"So, you don't believe in God."

"Why do you want me to believe in God? That isn't something for you to worry about. I am a bad girl and so be it."

"I have no such intentions whatsoever but sample this. Did you know that if Gravity were slightly more powerful, the Universe would collapse into a ball?"

"I did not, and I need not."

"And if the Gravity were a little less powerful, the Universe would fly apart. And there would be no stars or planets?"

"Where are you going with this?"

"It's just that Gravity is precisely as it needs to be. And if the ratio of the electromagnetic force to the strong force wasn't one percent, life wouldn't exist! What are the odds that all this would happen by itself."

Why are you trying to convince me to believe in God?

"The precision of the Universe at least makes it logical to conclude there's a Creator. There are eight billion people in this Universe. We met a few hours ago, and you seem like a perfect daughter to me. What are the odds of that?"

Shibra looked confused as Nuvem continued, "And do you think we both are here by accident? Sceptic persons, no doubt could attribute our pre-dawn meeting today during those dangerous circumstances to a freak occurrence, but was it a chance that I suddenly decided to drive to Fagu even under the influence of liquor and met you precisely at a place and time of your distress? Isn't that Weird?"

"Weird?"

"Yes, because in ancient times the word Weird was spelt as Wyrd. It's an Anglo-Saxon and Norse word. It means that everything in the Universe is connected by a weave of intricate strands. It is our fate and our destiny. Wyrd is said to be controlled by three sisters called the Norns, they are responsible for shaping our lives. Their names are 'Uror' – that which has become, 'Veroandi' – that which is in the process of becoming, and 'Skuld' – that which should be. Simply stating our destiny is all about our past, present, and future!

One ramification of Wyrd in personal human terms is that our past, both our ancestry and our personal history, affects us continually. Who we are, where we are, and what we are doing today is dependent on actions we have taken in the past and actions others have taken in the past which have affected us in some way. And every choice we make in the present builds upon choices we have previously made. Every day we are shaping our destiny and by the choices we make we are shaping others' destiny for generations to come. That all lives are connected by a web of fate."

"This is only an opinion based on our parenting and societal conditioning, and it is heavy stuff. The reality of the truth here is a suspect. But you never asked me about what I was doing and why I was doing it there?"

"I didn't ask you because I don't want you to relive your pain again and again and hurt yourself more in the process. I have been through the journey you are going through and I am now at a stage where I am learning to dance freely, with the wounds beneath my feet. I lost her some three years ago. And I knew no one could do anything to help me overcome my pain except me and myself. I believed there was a freak chance of a sane pulse of your faith that would get you back from the brink of emotional insanity, it surely did, and saved your life in the morning today. Probably my presence was mandated at that precise place and moment to witness that positive thought and I am eternally grateful for that thought, whatever it was, to which you paid heed."

"Perhaps that thought brought the face of my mother before me and she saved me once again. Now I understand the odds that out of eight billion people in this Universe she is my mother and I love her."

Joy of Dissatisfaction

"Don't plan too much, life has its own plans for you. Always remember that some of the most beautiful moments of your life are actually unplanned."

Nuvem was happy that Shibra was willing to speak and he asked, "Tell me why at that unearthly hour were you heading to Narkanda?"

Shibra had a kind of a lost look on her face and almost apologisingly she exclaimed, "Narkanda!" She was quiet for a moment pondering over the events of the previous night and embarrassingly admitted, "I was driving to Dehradun but, probably, coming from Naldehra, I took a wrong turn. This is our family problem. Barring my mom, none of us have a sense of direction."

Nuvem was wondering why she had to go to Dehradun so late into the night and that too in inclement weather conditions. He was quite intrigued that she took a wrong turn and they met. That meeting was definitely not an accident, it had a purpose! What could that be and why? But he only asked, "What's there in Naldehra?"

"We own a resort there. It was a much-loved go-to place for our family vacays. Oh, Naldehra is so beautiful. It is famous for its greenery, golf course, and plain view of mountains filled with pine, cedar, and deodar trees. With a backdrop of the mountains and the Sutlej River flowing through, Naldehra is breathtaking.

My father was an avid golfer and he loved to play at Naldehra Golf Course. Naldehra is a paradise for nature lovers and it is famous as one of the oldest golf courses in the country is located there at a height of 2,200 metres above sea level. An eighteen-hole course there is considered as one of the most challenging in India."

Shibra thought for a moment and then she suddenly asked, "Do you play golf?"

Nuvem smiled, "I knew this was coming. I don't play golf, golf plays me. More than the game, the lure of the lush green courses, hearty laughter of my friends, and sometimes their tears when hearts are laid bare, splintered tea-huts, blooming flowers and splatter of authentic colours of nature, rustling of leaves, occasionally nearly the impossible trajectory of the golf ball which goes through the branches of trees when it has no business of going there, and at times jumping on the surface of water bodies and landing on the greens, or jumping out of a deep bunker on to the green, and all the bad shots and good results, and coining unique words for appreciating a good shot, appeal to me.

My die-hard golfer friends think I am not a serious golfer. But I am serious about having fun in everything I do."

Nuvem paused for a moment and his thoughts drifted towards life. He said, that playing any sport is good because the beauty of all sports is that they reflect positive traits of life like patience, persistence, endurance, and excellence. Sports are meditative, like they say a good shooter holds her breath and fires the shot between the heartbeats, in the time interval between two consecutive beats of her heart. That's the effort life expects from us to be happy. But life is more beautiful than anything else in the world because we have no option of not playing even if the level playing fields are undulating and not as smooth as the playing grounds of sports. That makes the game of life more interesting than all the games people play.

The logic of 'Don't Play If You Can't Play' doesn't apply to life. Every sport comes closest to the game of life. It's a shadow of one's life and it's a healthy addiction that ends every day. You have choices on the play fields as in life, but you have no control whatsoever when it comes to the choices to choose from and fructification and otherwise of the chosen choices."

Shibra was looking at him silently and listening to him say what which was not making much sense to her. It was quite intriguing for her to note why all men talk too much about life, and wish they could live their lives with the same passion. Women that way are blessed because their basic instincts have been so constituted as to allow them to flow naturally with life without getting into prolonged dialogue towards understanding life or otherwise.

But she heard him patiently because she felt her father too wanted to talk about life sometimes and she never had the patience to hear him out. Today, when a stranger was saying the same things, she could understand why her father was so addicted to the game of golf.

When he found her engrossed with herself, Nuvem realised he was tormenting her with unnecessary heavy, and theoretical stuff. Nuvem felt that was a polite way to instigate dialogue within Shibra and thus empower her to address her inner turmoil more pragmatically. But he switched tracks, shifted to a more contemporary subject, and said, "Have you ever wondered that the addictive nature of unsatisfactory experience is always enjoyable."

Shibra's expression was like what, "The joy of dissatisfaction!!!"

"This is Dorito Theory, popularised by social media user Celeste Aria in a viral video, that explains the addictive nature of unsatisfying experiences. It suggests that experiences like eating Doritos chips are maximally addictive because the peak satisfaction is during consumption, not afterwards. Happiness resides more in the journey than the destination, the destination is fixed; the journey continues till eternity. It should make sense to make the journey itself the destination!

This theory, viewed over one million times, applies to addictive behaviours like doomscrolling, gambling, and junk food binging. It aligns with reinforcement theory, stating that occasional rewards fuel addiction. Understanding this concept sheds light on how modern habits and behaviours intertwine with psychological theories, prompting deeper reflections on our digital consumption patterns and the nature of addiction in contemporary society."

"You mean my pain too is a joy of dissatisfaction?"

"As per the Dorito Theory, even life is a joy of dissatisfaction! As I have said earlier, every happy moment is a positive addiction, but pain is negative and morbid. Whether Dorito's theory applies to pain or not, I won't know but most of us who have suffered the loss of a loved one view the negative process of healing as a means to honour our departed loved ones. That's an illusion of the positivity of negativity. Having said that, I feel the celebration of their lives is a positive process of honouring them and you can only celebrate them by celebrating yourself. And that there should be no place for the occurrences like today morning's madness."

Nuvem did not want the conversation to turn in that direction as yet and he said, "It is already 3:00 P.M. weather seems to be packing up, so, let's cut the interesting conversation short and hurry back home before the rains catch up with us."

The descent was quiet and they reached back in thirty minutes. By that time even her car fetched up. They had a hot cup of coffee and sandwiches before retiring to their rooms. Their party was due in the evening. Purpose and the beautiful weather had to meet.

Real Eyes, Real Lies, Realise

"We see the world, not as it is, but as we are – or, as we are conditioned to see it. When we open our mouths to describe what we see, we in effect describe ourselves, our perceptions, our paradigms."

– Stephen R. Covey

Nuvem came to his room and he still found it difficult to push the image of the lanky silhouette of Shibra teetering on the road protection concrete barrier out of his mind. The picture kept coming back to him every time he tried to take his mind away from it. That was a classic case of the fear of an imaginary negative outcome and human helplessness in the inevitability of the unforeseen.

Nuvem was wondering whether we are all on a mass head trip and in this age of magical overthinking, our minds have turned against us. True, magical thinking is an age-old trait and our minds have always been resource-rational, using shortcuts to process information. But today, a sudden and extreme information load, loneliness, urban angst, noise of all kinds, virtual and literal, and capitalist pressure to know everything are causing our thought patterns to go haywire. Cognitive biases, which were our ancestors' mental cheat codes, are now causing us to overthink or underthink the wrong things. Our minds have turned against us, truly …

Anyway, he was grossly shaken to the core of his being by the real possibility of a very likely tragic outcome of an emotional turmoil that could claim the life of a young woman that morning and her reasons would have died with her as well.

But who is Shibra Salim after all? Why is he so concerned about a stranger whom he met that morning itself? Was a bond in making between them? What bond? A bond of pain, perhaps! Why was he seeing his daughter in her? As an ex-Army man, suicide will always be a cowardly act for him. An utterly dishonourable act. But things suddenly took a turn for the worse in his life and shook his fundamentals and his entire belief system.

Immense pain in his life had surely made him much more empathetic, compassionate, and caring. He had understood that sometimes people with mental troubles run out of options and suicidal tendencies come to the fore as an honourable option to end one's pain. But pain doesn't end, it only gets magnified with the end of one's life in a sense their loved ones have to bear that burden of pain also for the rest of their lives. Most of the time, that will be a double whammy of pain!

But why didn't he ask her about it though she was willing to talk about it? He should have allowed her to vent her feelings to lighten herself. Wasn't he being insensitive to her mental condition or was he supporting her by not talking about her weaker moments? Whatever that was, Nuvem had no clue or control of what exactly he was doing.

And that triggered another bout with his deeper thoughts. Nuvem was constantly trying to save himself from his habit of deep thinking as a defence mechanism for the management of his anguish and pain. But that day he couldn't help drifting into those negative thoughts which by now had become familiar patterns of his mind in distress.

We are paradoxical. We like to be happy but we think sad things all the time. We don't really like ourselves, but we love the person we have become. We say we don't care but we care too much deep into our bones. We crave attention yet we reject everything that comes our way. We try to heal others while breaking ourselves all the time. We love to speak but never listen.

Who are we? Do we even know us?

All men contain several men inside them, and most of us bounce from one self to another without ever knowing who we are! Different versions of our lives play out to different ends as an act of faith. This entanglement must assume an investigation of identity, love, and loss and what remains when old certainties give way.

There are curiosities in life that fuel fiction. So many strange things happen in our lives, so many unexpected and improbable events that we can no longer be certain whether we know what reality is anymore. Yet we aren't prepared to expect the unexpected in our lives.

We find ourselves against a wall of our own making and then find we cannot find a way around it. Later, we, with dazed, faraway eyes and clouded minds, would struggle to put words to the events, a series of strange episodes that will invariably follow.

Every story of life is fiction, of course, and, therefore, they tell lies (in the strictest sense of the term), but through those lies, every one of us tries to understand the truth about the world.

A different version of us exists in the minds of everyone who knows us. But the problem is no one really knows us!

The person we think of as "ourself" exists only for us, one version at a time, and even we don't really know who that is. Every person we meet, have a relationship with, or make eye contact on the street with, creates a version of "us" in their heads.

We are not the same person to our mom, our dad, or our siblings as we are to our coworkers, our neighbours, or our friends. There are a thousand different versions of ourselves out there, in people's minds. A "me" exists in each version, and yet my "me", isn't really a "someone" at all.

So, we are actually faking the person we are. If everything and everyone becomes spurious the bogus becomes the bona fide. And that way we tell lies about ourselves, and don't even realise with our real eyes that we are deeply fake.

Maybe the journey isn't so much about becoming anything. Maybe it's about un-becoming everything that isn't really us, so we can be who we are meant to be in the first place.

The Quantum Law of Being states that reality is like a mirror that reflects on us. Based on our inner state of being, it suggests that the external world is not completely separate and independent from our inner world of thoughts, feelings, and beliefs. It is more about both a flower and its fragrance.

The external world responds to and reflects our internal state. If we believe ourselves to be stuck in life, the world will prove us right and reflect stuckness back to us. But if we assume the state of being free even before the outer conditions change, the world will begin to reflect back more freedom and opportunities. Essentially, we shape reality based on who we believe ourselves to be.

By changing our inner state, our assumptions, thoughts, and feelings, we cause the mirror of reality to morph and transform accordingly. The world depends on us, observers, to determine which timeline of infinite possibilities manifests. We are the masters of our fate and captains of our ships. And that's the problem. The quantum field responds to our consciousness and mirrors back to us our state of being, which we are not very sure of.

No matter how old, wise, and psychologically sorted we feel, there are times when we get trapped in emotional mayhem. We feel horrible, ruminate over our irrational thoughts and end up engaging ourselves in dysfunctional behaviours – the reactions which we regret later, like the one he witnessed in the morning.

But at that moment, no reasoning or intervention seems to assuage our pain. Although we often believe that negative emotions arise within us in response to painful external stimuli, that is far from the truth. In fact, there is a part of our mind that always plays a very active role in creating and perpetuating those emotions. It's a permanent DNA defect, perhaps.

Neuropsychological research has proven that most emotions are naturally programmed to last no more than ninety seconds. If we feel anger, envy, grief, or sadness for minutes, hours, days, months, or years, it simply indicates that we are doing something actually to re-stimulate the negative emotional circuit and falling into the mayhem of our suffering again and again.

Let's imagine we are driving on the road and a motorist nearly bumps into us. We feel intense anger and this anger stays for a few seconds before automatically dissipating. But before this anger can dissipate, we focus all our attention on our pain and think about it repeatedly. We recall past pain, traumas, and unfortunate experiences produce new angry feelings and continually injure our thoughts in the present moment. Our self-dialogue runs on these lines, "Why I'm destined to receive such nuisance in all spheres of my life? Why do people always trouble me? Why does everyone take advantage of my niceness? Wait, this has to stop and I need to teach everyone a lesson." And this self-dialogue ensures that our anger is kept alive and simmering.

It continues to show us the replays of our pain to the extent we start to like our victimhood. It gives us a sense of being separated from ourselves and fuels and authenticates such painful feelings repeatedly. And our thoughts become the carriers of such feelings deep within us and our hearts and minds fight with each other. Our minds and hearts must befriend themselves as soon as possible to alleviate our painful feelings. Self-help is the only way to our freedom.

Fortunately, Nuvem had consciously decided to discipline his inner realm to the extent that he was able to maintain a fragile external equilibrium in his being. He had understood that to transcend this situation, he needed to stop justifying his reactions and shift his focus away from the emotional baggage that he was carrying. He had to look for new patterns to deal with his feelings so that he could stop creating repetitive chaos in his new existence.

This redemption of sorts took almost three years to make some sense in his mind with an explicit acceptance that the process will never be complete. Time heals, but it cannot delete what has already happened. One has no right to be forgotten by his pain. And that's an advantage as well because our pain renews us and it is the way to remember and honour our loved ones who have left us although they still live within us in the presence of their absence. His life was undulating like a sine wave where pain and happiness cancelled each other out to grant him a fragile feeling of neutrality and new normality. But he had to replace his pain with happiness as a way to honour Vrishti.

To him personally, the starting point was achieving stability in his breath. The conscious breathing certainly helped him to rediscover balance and rhythms in his life. Once we learn to control our breath, we learn to control our sympathetic and parasympathetic nervous systems, which in turn helps us regulate our emotional reactions better.

And what if reactions, good, bad, or indifferent are invited by our destiny? It is as weird as it could be. That's why the meaning of the original word "Wyrd" is destiny. To be weird one follows the path of their destiny meaning that normal is a clear road that has been paved and when you are weird, no one can show you the way.

And when all of us are weird, what is destiny? Does it cease to have a meaning? We have been conditioned to believe that a dream is only worthy if we can realise, actualise, and monetise it. However, we are oblivious to the fact that beyond a point, a monetised dream can quickly turn into a nightmare. But what if our dreams are not random, what if they choose us as much as we choose them and we owe it again to destiny that we have that bond?

With so many ifs and buts it is quite obvious that our destiny is not our work. To hustle for our purpose, we must have a to-do list and a way to check off that list so we don't feel worthless.

Our destiny is not to find the one and fall in love, and create a family, but to keep falling in love again and yet again with someone or something until death decides to come. Destiny will reveal the path to us with every step we take. But steps we must take because action is the essence of life.

So, keep going even if there's nowhere to arrive. Keep loving and creating. Keep rising and falling and hoping and dreaming. Our lungs were the first thing God kissed when we came into this world. So, every inhale and exhale is a love story of purpose, weird like the one that is on the path of our destiny.

But destiny cannot be a convenient excuse and one-stop solution that fits all. Destiny comes into play only when we have no answers to some of the questions life throws at us. This in a way is good because destiny then brings much-needed acceptance into our lives.

After his NDA Course Get Together at Narkanda, Nuvem decided to have a stopover at Fagu to sample some ideas for his next book. Like most of his travel plans that was an impromptu decision. In his experience, an unplanned physics of his quest always organised his thoughts to experiment with finding happiness beyond the tunnel of his sadness for the untimely loss of his love.

Everything was okay till then, he was in his happiness zone, even listening to Taylor Swift, and then he saw Shibra Salim preparing to take a plunge into the valley of her death. That sight and its horrible potential perturbed him and pushed him back into an unfamiliar territory of his loneliness. An unknown territory where he always struggled with his unsavoury and philosophically charged thoughts from where he could only reach nowhere but into a web of the very same suffering which he wanted to overcome.

Fractured Solitude

"Find me where the crowd is less, the sky is blue, and the wind is free. Find me in the midst of the forgotten: the abandoned. To the one who seeks my presence, find me in the company of the unseen."

– the_written_journey

Shibra returned to her room and just slept, a sound two hours of recuperative sleep. She woke up when Keenie Bhai brought piping hot coffee and her favourite coconut cookies. She enjoyed her coffee after a long time and it brightened up her evening. Shibra was keen to talk a lot of things with Nuvem. She wanted to know the source from which he drew strength to be so calm and strong. She wanted to know the code of his happiness. She had decided to find peace within herself and was willing to go ahead in life. She wanted to take stock of their family business and most importantly she wanted her mother's love to bless her. Is love the code of happiness?

But she somehow felt, Nuvem was a little hesitant to open up to her. In the afternoon that day, he only talked around the peripheral issues, as if he was trying to probe the fragility of her mind. That sounded logical as well because they were strangers who just met. "But what about those vibes between them?", pondered Shibra.

Nuvem was comfortably sitting in the drawing room and Shibra was still riding the waves of her thoughts in her room. Nuvem was aware that Shibra was battling difficult times in her life. She was strong, but lost her rudder with the demise of her dad. She trusted him but Nuvem had no idea how to come up to her expectations, or whether it was possible to come to the expectations of his fellow human. Is shared humanity a guiding force for human relationships? He accepted that an unidentifiable and nameless relationship of pure affection was surely building between them. And why was he worrying so much about her?

She is a child of God and He will test her many more times to make her what He wants her to become. Spanish phrase, Lo Que Sera, Sera means What Will be, Will Be. In the lyrics of a famous song, a young girl asks her mother about the future and whether she will be pretty or rich. "Que sera, sera ... Her mother replies, "... the future's not ours to see ... whatever will be, will be."

Lost in those thoughts, Nuvem was waiting for Shibra when she came and greeted him. The drawing room was lavishly organised and aesthetically lit. But the real beauty was a contrasting stark darkness outside where the falling snowflakes and warmth of the room combined to wrap the large window glasses with an illusion of the due of the morning. That was a kind of morning into the evening! Nuvem was sipping cognac and Shibra joined him with some hot water.

Shibra was quite prepared not to allow Nuvem to skirt the issue any further and she came to the point straightway "What made you overcome your grief and reach out to your daughters? How did you manage to let Vrishti Ma'am go?

Nuvem smiled, the smile that veiled his feeling that the young woman was expecting the solution from someone while it was resting within herself. That was quite like the musk deer! There was a longish pause after her question because Nuvem was sure both her questions were incorrect. He wasn't even sure whether he was right in his judgement.

Shibra waited patiently when he spoke, "I haven't overcome my grief, it will never go, and I want it for it represents my love for my Vrishti. I will not even let her go, and it is not possible to let her go because she has already gone. So, I have to let something else go. Having said that, I must say I am in transition and much better now in accepting my state of unhappiness more cheerfully.

But the story doesn't begin here. It begins when grief relents its intensity and loneliness gatecrashes in life. Loneliness is the beginning of the process of coming to terms with oneself. So, let's talk about loneliness to welcome a new normal in our lives. I prefer to call positive loneliness a fractured solitude because it breaks my solitude at random and yet gives a positive connotation to my fragility and hope that it is possible to find myself for me despite being alone. In the hierarchy of management of my emotions, the state of being alone is an acceptable balance between loneliness and solitude. Aloneness is a positive loneliness, it's a state above loneliness and below solitude. Aloneness is a fractured solitude!

Nuvem paused for a moment and observed perplexity on Shibra's innocent face. She looked at him in his eyes when he asked, "Tell me what is loneliness?"

Shibra took some time and replied, "It's a state of being alone."

Nuvem politely but immediately checked her and said, "No, no Loneliness is not being alone. Single life is a vibe.

Alone is not boring like loneliness. It is so peaceful. Some people come into our lives just to teach us how to live alone, not lonely. So, let's define loneliness to understand the root cause of the problem and find a workable solution.

Loneliness is a state of mind. It's a kind of mental or emotional discomfort one experiences and it is a universal phenomenon and sonder. It makes one feel empty and unwanted. Lonely people often crave human contact, but the fragile state of their minds makes it more difficult to form connections with others."

Shibra was listening quietly and she was surprised why she was craving to connect with Nuvem. She was sorely missing her father. She didn't feel the urge to connect with her mother till Nuvem compelled her to think of her in the morning and she innocently asked, "What is the main cause of loneliness?"

Nuvem smiled at the interesting irony where one lonely girl was asking another lonely guy, both lonely and even aware of why they were lonely. Interestingly again, the relationships woven in pain form instant and genuine bonds between humans. But ironies have no place in empathy. He replied, "Both of us are grieving the loss of our loved ones and we are lonely. In your case, there may be many more reasons like life changes or circumstances that include living alone, changing your living arrangements, failure, or having financial problems, etc. that caused loneliness.

In the same breath, he asked, "Based on your experience, what would you say, is loneliness an illness, or is it a feeling?"

"I am not sure, at first, if loneliness could be classified as an illness. If you stick by the definition of illness being "an unhealthy state of the body or mind" then you have your answer right there. To me, it doesn't matter if it is self-inflicted or not, occurring in awareness or not ... how can so many people be lonely? Is this the default state of human nature, or is it only a side effect of cognitive impairments? I'm not sure, but my experience says that loneliness itself can kill, typically by raising blood pressure and increasing the risk of heart disease and stroke. Or maybe, it's not loneliness that can kill, but it is how a person perceives his or her situation that matters more. My psychologist told me that people can live alone and still have great affiliations with friends and family. However, in my case, I can live among several others, but with no real connections."

"I somehow am convinced that loneliness could lead to life-threatening diseases, per se it is only a feeling, a dangerous feeling at that. Therefore, the way you regard your situation is crucial in battling this feeling. While it is an unavoidable human condition one is confronted with, one can also take it as a great opportunity for self-awareness and truth; perhaps for some people, a little bit of loneliness is beneficial.

Millions of people experience this feeling which only serves to alienate oneself from others. Loneliness is a feeling, not necessarily a fact of our existence – especially if we decide we don't want it to be. Let's try not to let our negatively perceived situations become the basis of our feelings because loneliness can, expeditiously and needlessly, kill us, or destroy our happiness and that of those who love us and whom we must love. I can't think of a better reason to start becoming the type of person who can truly enjoy his or her own company.

While experiencing loneliness, we often underestimate the beauty of serendipity, overshadowed by our intense focus on curated experiences. This fixation leaves us uncomfortable in the spontaneity of life's moments."

"Is there a difference between depression and loneliness?"

"I feel they are essentially the same and the only difference being that depression is an extreme form of loneliness. Both must be overcome but the degree of difficulty to defeat depression is much more than overcoming loneliness. So, one should seek expert advice to reach manageable levels from where our willpower can come into play to make us feel better."

Nuvem looked at Shibra, thought something, and continued, "The crux is to dance freely, with the wound beneath our feet. Loneliness should not be a memoir of grievance, but sharp gratitude for life. It asks for neither pity nor awe. The remedial act is compassion. We need to give meaning to our pain and suffering to remind ourselves that life can never be silenced while living. I feel all the sorrows of life are bearable if only we can convert them into a story. The only reasonable response for a difficult fate is that we may laugh at it, with it. We have to exhort ourselves to come back and go dancing to the newer tunes of life."

A Cat and Mouse Game

"I like scars because I like stories. Bravery, stupidity, pain – none of them come free."

– Jessica Martinez, Virtuosity

When Shibra returned to her room after dinner, she pondered over their conversation on loneliness and depression for a while. In doing so she touched a wrong chord unwittingly. She felt lonely and after a while, she was in the grip of now familiar restlessness once again. Those two stalkers, loneliness and depression, were lurking outside the cottage. She saw them through the fog outside the window. She was surprised they didn't break into her room. She felt protected.

Was that because of the assuring presence of her dad in Nuvem? What she liked in Nuvem was, like her father who never recounted her blunders, he didn't ask anything of what blunder she was about to make in the morning. Or was he being insensitive to her pain? After all, he was just a stranger whom she just met that morning itself. She quickly shrugged off the unpleasant thought because she knew she felt safe in his company.

And once assured that those two goons couldn't enter her room, she recollected their latest violation of her emotional modesty which led her to the latest bout of extreme uneasiness that caused the near disastrous episode of that morning. She felt she was losing control once again. She was soon complaining to herself and reflecting on how things got out of her hands and pushed her into her latest misadventure in the emotional minefield.

Shibra was so ashamed of her pre-dawn grave indiscretion because of which she came dangerously close to ending her life by suicide. During those distressing moments, she had almost forfeited her sanity. Nuvem was God sent and he was surely becoming her Blue because, in his comforting company, she realised that finding the traces of happiness in life was the way forward for getting rid of her loneliness and depression. She replayed the scenario that got her back to almost taking her life that day. That was one of the darkest phases of her life and she had to see light to get out of it.

She remembered depression and loneliness tracked her down after about ten days in Naldehra. She was walking through the countryside that evening after a happy day spent in their resort, and the sun was setting gold over the mountain. She felt good in that romantic setting, even if she was all by herself, while everyone else in the vast field at the sunset point was either cosying up with a lover or playing with a laughing child. She stopped to lean against a balustrade and watch the sunset, and she got to thinking a little too much, and then her thinking turned to brooding, and that's when they caught up with her.

They came upon her all silent and menacing like wicked men, and they flanked her – Depression on her left, Loneliness on her right. They didn't need to reveal their identity or introduce themselves; she knew those guys very well. They have been playing a hide-and-seek game for almost three years now. Though she admitted that she was surprised to meet them in that elegant place at dusk. That was no place they belonged.

She said to them, "How did you find me here? Who told you I had come to Naldehra?"

Depression, always the wily guy said, "What – you're not happy to see us?"

"Go away," she protested helplessly.

Loneliness, a little more considerate guy, said, "I am sorry little lady. But I might have to tail you the whole time you're travelling. It gives me a lot of pleasure."

"I'd really rather you didn't," she told him, and he shrugged almost apologetically, but only moved closer.

Then they frisked her and violated her privacy and every sense of her peace with herself. They emptied her bag of any joy she had been carrying there. Depression even snatched away her identity, but he always did that.

Then Loneliness started questioning her, which she dreaded because it would go on for hours. He was polite but persistent, and he always made her feel miserable in the end. He asked her if she had any reason to be happy that she knew of. He asked her why she was all by herself that evening, yet again. He asked (though they've been through this line of questioning hundreds of times already) why she had messed up things with Shameer, why she messed things up with everyone around her, including herself. He asked her why she couldn't get her act together and accept the passing away of her dad, and why she was not home taking care of her lonely mom. He also reminded her how she neglected her mom, didn't call her for days, and even disconnected her calls by pretending to be busy. He asked her why, exactly, she thought she deserved a vacation in Naldehra when she had made such a rubble of her life. He asked her why she thought that running away from home would make her happy. He asked her where she thought she would end up in her life if she kept living that way.

She walked back to her hut, hoping to shake them, but they kept following her, those two goons. Depression had a firm hand on her shoulder and Loneliness harangued her with his interrogation. She didn't even bother eating dinner; she didn't want them watching her. She didn't want to let them in her room, either, but she knew Depression, and he had got a gun, so there's no stopping him from coming in if he decided that he wanted to.

"It's not fair for you to come here," she told Depression, "I paid you off already. I served my time at Club Eleven, a psychic facility back in both Delhi and Dehradun."

But he just gave her that dark smile, settled into her favourite chair, put his feet on her table, and lighted a cigarette, filling the place with his awful smell and smoke. Loneliness watched and sighed, then climbed into her bed and pulled the cover over himself, fully dressed, shoes and all. He was going to make her sleep with him again that night, she just knew it.

She'd stopped taking her medication only a few weeks earlier. It just seemed crazy to be taking antidepressants in Naldehra. How could she be depressed there?

She'd never wanted to be on medication in the first place. She'd fought taking it for so long, mainly because of a long list of personal objections (e.g.: Indians are overmedicated; we don't know the long-term effects of this stuff yet on the human brain; it's a crime that even Indian children are on antidepressants these days; we are treating the symptoms and not the causes of the mental health conditions …) Still during the last two years of her life, there was no question that she was in grave trouble and that trouble was not lifting quickly. As her dad died of that sudden cardiac arrest and her drama with Shameer evolved, she'd come to have all the symptoms of major depression – loss of sleep, appetite and libido, uncontrollable weeping, chronic backaches and stomachaches, alienation and despair, trouble concentrating on work, inability to even get upset with any and everything … it went on and on.

When you were lost in those woods, it sometimes took you a while to realise that you were lost. For the longest time, you could convince yourself that you'd just wandered a few feet off the path and that you'd find your way back to the trailhead any moment now. Then night fell again and again, and you still had no idea where you were, and it was time to admit that you had bewildered yourself so far off the path that you didn't even know from which direction the sun rose anymore.

She took on her depression like it was the fight of her life, which, of course, it was. She became a student of her own depressed existence, trying to unearth its causes. What was the root of all that despair? Was it psychological? (It was not her fault.) Was it temporal, a 'bad time' in her life? Was it general melancholy? (Habitually watching sad reels on Instagram and listening to sad songs.) Was it cultural? (Indian girl trying to find balance in an increasingly stressful and alienating urban world.) Was it artistic? (Intelligent and talented girls always suffered from depression because they were supersensitive and special.) Was it evolutionary? (Did she carry in her the residual panic that came after millennia of her species' attempting to survive a brutal world?) Was it karmic? (Were all those spasms of grief just the consequences of bad behaviour in previous lifetimes, the last obstacles before liberation?) Was it hormonal? Dietary? Philosophical? Seasonal? Environmental? Was she tapping into a universal yearning for God? (Which she herself never believed.) Did she have a chemical imbalance? Or did she just need to relax? Wasn't she trying enough? Why was she not surrendering to God Almighty?

What a large number of factors constituted a single human being! How very many layers we operated on, and how very many influences we received from our minds, our bodies, our histories, our families, our cities, and our souls. She came to feel that her depression was probably because of her inability to cope with the sudden loss of her father, the removal of her support system without his assuring presence in her life, narcissism of Shameer Sikander who was the coward who awakened her love with no intention of loving her, her unexplainable indifference towards the silent suffering of her mother who lost her husband, probably some ever-shifting assortment of all those factors, and probably also included some stuff she couldn't name or claim. So, she faced fight and flight at every level.

She tried so hard to fight the endless sobbing. She remembered asking herself one night, while she was curled up in the same old corner of her couch in tears yet again over the same old repetition of sorrowful thoughts, "Was there anything about that scene you could change, Shibra?" And all she could think to do was to stand up on the balcony of her room, while still sobbing, and try to calm herself down unsuccessfully. Just to prove that – while she couldn't stop the tears or change her dismal internal dialogue – she was not yet totally out of control: at least she could cry hysterically while standing on her balcony, and that too without any dark thoughts. That was the start.

She crossed the street to walk in the sunshine. She tried to lean on her support network, cherishing her family, especially her mom, and cultivating her most enlightening friendships. But her low self-esteem wasn't helping depression matters at all, she got herself a pretty haircut, bought some fancy makeup, and a nice dress. That was the beginning of "Operation Restart Her Life." She also hired the services of an online psychologist from Jalandhar and she loved talking to her. The best thing about her psychologist was she loved to listen to her and then say some words hearing them from her made sense to Shibra and more importantly they made her feel so much better.

The last thing she tried, after about two years of fighting that sorrow, was medication. If she might impose her opinions here, she thought that should always be the last thing anyone tried. For her, the decision to go the route of anti-depressants happened after a night when she sat on the floor of her bedroom for many hours, trying very hard to talk herself out of cutting into her wrist with a blade.

She won the argument against the blade that night, but barely. She had some other good ideas around that time – about how jumping off the balcony of her ninth-floor flat or jumping in front of a metro train might stop the suffering. But something about spending a night with a blade in her hand did it. Would the latest deadly misadventure of the morning liberate her from such dangerous choices in the future? She was hopeful, it would.

Recognise Yourself as Your Friend

"This is what I believe: That I am I. That my soul is a dark forest. That my known self will never be more than a little clearing in the forest. That Gods, strange Gods, come forth from the forest into the clearing of my known self and then go back. That I must have the courage to let them come and go. That I will never let mankind put anything over me, but that I will always try to recognise and submit to the Gods in me and the Gods in other men and women. There is my creed."

– DH Lawrence

The next morning, she called her friend Sarla as the sun came up, and begged her to help her. She didn't think a woman in the whole history of her family had ever done that before, had ever sat down in the middle of the road like that and said, in the middle of her life, "I cannot walk another step further – someone has to help me."

And she would never forget Sarla's face when she rushed into her bedroom about an hour after her emergency phone call and saw her in a heap on her bed. The image of her pain mirrored back at her through Sarla's visible fear for her life was still one of the scariest memories for her out of all those scary years. She huddled in a ball while Sarla made the phone calls and found her a psychiatrist who would give her a consultation that very day, to discuss the possibility of prescribing antidepressants. She listened to Sarla's one-sided conversation with the doctor, and listened to her say, "I'm afraid my friend is going to seriously hurt herself." She was afraid, too.

When she went to see the psychiatrist that afternoon, the doctor asked her what had taken her so long to get help – as if she hadn't been trying to help herself already for so long. She told the doctor her objections and reservations about antidepressants. She requested her to not do anything to harm her brain. The psychiatrist said, "If you had sprained your ankle or twisted your knee, you wouldn't hesitate to take medication for it – why are you hesitating with this?"

The doctor put her on a few different drugs until they found the combination that didn't make her nauseated or turn her libido into a dim and distant memory. She advised her not to go to work and instructed Sarla not to leave her alone for at least a month. Now that was an issue. She was putting in extra hours just to escape the prison of her notoriously negative thoughts. She didn't say anything to the psychiatrist but she knew she would not heed her advice about her work. Sarla knew that and she didn't oppose it either.

Quickly, in less than a week, she could feel an extra inch of daylight opening in her mind. Also, she could finally sleep. And that was the real gift because when you could not sleep, you could not get yourself out of the pit – there was not a chance. The pills gave her those recuperative night hours back and also stopped her hands from shaking and released the Vise grip around her chest and the panic alert button from inside her heart.

Still, she never felt comfortable taking those drugs, though they helped immediately. It never mattered who told her those medications were a good idea and perfectly safe; she always felt conflicted about that. Those drugs were part of her bridge to the safer side, there was no question about that, but she wanted to be off them as soon as possible. She started taking the medication in January of 2023. By September, she was already diminishing her dosage significantly. Those had been the toughest months, anyhow – the last months of her worst mood swings, the last ragged months of her obsession with Shameer. Could she have endured that time without drugs, if she'd just held out a little longer? Could she have survived herself, by herself? She didn't know. That was the thing about human life – there was no control group, no way to ever know how any of us would have turned out if any variables had been changed.

She did know those drugs made her misery feel less catastrophic. So, she was grateful for that. But she was still deeply ambivalent about mood-altering medications. She was awed by their power, but concerned by their prevalence, especially their presence in her life. She would think they needed to be prescribed and used with much more restraint, and never without the parallel treatment of psychological counselling. Medicating the symptoms of any illness without exploring its root cause was just a classically harebrained way to think that anyone could get truly better. Those pills might have saved her life, but they did so only in conjunction with about twenty other efforts she was making simultaneously during the same period to rescue herself, and she hoped to never have to take such drugs again. However, her doctor did suggest that she might have to go on and off antidepressants many times in her life because of her "tendency towards melancholy." She hoped to God the doctor was wrong. She intended to do everything she could to prove her wrong, or at least to fight that melancholic tendency with every tool in the shed – regular exercise regimen, balanced diet, restrain, patience, self-control, swimming, trekking, running half-marathons, meditation, prayers, etc. Whether that made her self-defeating stubborn, or self-preserving stubborn, she could not say though she could convincingly conclude living a simple life was a function of discipline.

But it was not difficult. As for her mental health, she was really creating a space in her routine for herself, to create the joy she hadn't seen in over three years. She had to prove to herself that she could go around the world, watch Netflix every once in a while, and wear her pyjamas.

But there she was.

"Or, rather- here I'm." Shibra reminded herself, "I'm in Fagu, and I'm still not out of trouble, but I feel safe here. Depression and Loneliness have barged into my life again, followed me to Fagu, and I just took my last tablet five days ago. There are more pills in my bag, but I don't want them. I want to be free of them forever. But I don't want Depression or Loneliness around either, so, I don't know what to do, and I am spiralling in panic, like I always spiral when I don't know what to do. So, what I do for tonight is to reach for myself, which I do when I am troubled by my vicious thoughts."

She opened up directly and said, "I need your help."

Then she waited. After a little while, a response came, in a strange voice, "I'm right here. What can I do for you? God has entrusted you with me."

And there recommenced her strangest and most secret conversation. There, in the most private moments, where she talked to herself. She talked to the same strange voice which by then had become very friendly and reassuring. In the months since she first accessed that suddenly in some difficult moments, she had found that voice again in times of code-red distress, and had learnt that the best way for her to reach that was in her conversation with herself. She had been surprised to find that she could almost always access that voice, too, no matter how black her anguish might be. Even during the worst of suffering, that calm, compassionate, affectionate, and infinitely wise voice (who may be her, or maybe not exactly her) was always available for a conversation at any time of the day or night.

She had decided to let herself off the hook from worrying that conversing with herself meant she was a schizo. Maybe the voice she was reaching for was God, or maybe it was her dad speaking through her, or maybe it was an angel who was assigned to her case, or maybe it was her higher self, or maybe it was indeed just a construct of her subconscious, invented in order to protect her from her own torment. One spiritual man called such divine internal voices, "locutions" – words from the supernatural that entered the mind spontaneously, translated into her own language, and offered her heavenly consolations. She knew what Freud would have said about such spiritual consolations, of course, that, "They are irrational and deserve no trust. Experience teaches us that the world is no nursery." She agreed – the world isn't a nursery. But the very fact that this world is so challenging is exactly why you sometimes must reach out to its jurisdiction for help, appealing to a higher authority to find your comfort. That's what even Nuvem had told her at Deshu Mata Temple at Fagu Top and that made more sense to her now.

At the beginning of her spiritual experiment, she didn't always have such faith in that internal voice of wisdom. Many a time of her moments of crises, in a bitter fury of rage and sorrow, she shouted at her inner voice, to her divine interior comfort, "I do not believe in you!!!"

After a moment, still breathing heavily, she felt a clear pinpoint of light ignite within her, and then she found herself getting this amused and ever-calm reply, "Who are you talking to, then?"

She hadn't doubted its existence again since. So, that night at Fagu, she reached for that voice again. That was the first time she had done that since she came to Naldehra. What she said to herself was that she was weak and full of fear. She explained that Depression and Loneliness had shown up, and she was scared they would never leave. She said that she didn't want to take the drugs anymore, but she was frightened she would have to. She was terrified that she would never really pull her life together.

In response, somewhere from within her, rose a now-familiar presence, offering her all the certainties she had always wished another person would say to her when she was troubled. That is what her inner voice said, "I'm here. I love you. I don't care if you need to stay up crying all night long. I will stay with you. If you need the medication again, go ahead and take it – I will love you through that, as well. If you don't need the medication, I will love you, too. There's nothing you can ever do to lose my love. I will protect you until you die, and after your death, I will still protect you. I am stronger than

Depression and I am braver than Loneliness and nothing will ever exhaust me."

That night, that strange gesture of friendship – the lending of a hand from her to herself when nobody else was around to offer solace – reminded her of something that happened to her once in New Delhi. She walked into an office building one afternoon in a hurry and dashed into the waiting elevator. As she rushed in, she caught an unexpected glimpse of herself in a security mirror's reflection.

She avoided her gaze in the mirror; She had no intention of learning what that felt like to meet her eyes. However, when she looked at them, she read sadness in them, and for a moment she was afraid … could they read hers?

In that moment of confusion, she decided to look into the mirror and her brain did an odd thing – it fired off this split-second message, "Hey! You know her! That's a friend of yours!" And she actually ran forward towards her own reflection with a smile, ready to welcome that girl whose name she had lost but whose face was so familiar. In a flash instant, of course, she realised her mistake and laughed in embarrassment at her almost doglike confusion over how a mirror worked. But for some reason that incident came to her mind again during her sadness at Fagu. She found herself saying this comforting reminder, "Never forget that once upon a time, in an unguarded moment, you recognised yourself as a friend."

She fell asleep holding her pillow pressed against her chest, open to this most recent assurance. In the morning when she woke up, she could still smell a faint trace of Depression's lingering smoke, but he himself was nowhere to be seen. Somewhere during the night, he got up and left. And buddy

Loneliness beat it, too. How she wish she never have to meet them again!

She felt very light and refreshed. Just then, Keenie Bhai knocked on her door. The hot cup of ginger tea with rusks was the most welcome sight in that awfully cold morning at Fagu.

Cry But Never Forget to Laugh

"Finish each day and be done with it. You have done what you could. Some blunders and absurdities no doubt have crept in; forget them as soon as you can. Tomorrow is a new day. You shall begin it serenely and with too high a spirit to be encumbered with your old nonsense."

– Ralph Waldo Emerson

A little later, Shibra freshened up and draped a shawl over her otherwise warm casual outfit as she walked into the large drawing room of their cottage. It was awfully cold out there and it was snowing outside. Keenie Bhai was waiting for her with a large umbrella to lead her to the Sunroom where Nuvem was waiting for her. They walked on a slab stone pathway specially constructed over the slippery ground, with the cleared snow accumulated on either side of it, into the room. An intensely lit fireplace and hearth had heated the room cosy, creating a relaxing ambience that instantly warmed up her heart. The room was aesthetically designed to harness the ultraviolet rays of the sun to combat the cold of Fagu and had a tastefully done interior and comfortable seating. It was a beautiful glass house with the inner and ceiling lining of slidable rich curtains. The whole get-up was simply pure class. But the sun did not show up that morning and it hid behind a thick layer of cloud cover.

Nuvem was sitting comfortably by the side of the fireplace with a soft blanket spread over his legs. He greeted her warmly, adjusted himself on the sofa, and welcomed her to a similar seating arrangement in front of the hearth. Keenie served her a hot cup of tea with some cookies.

The whole setting of the Sunroom was quite luxurious and it reflected a fine aesthetic taste of the Bhasins. Shibra instantly connected to the way her father loved such cosy corners while complaining all the time there weren't any pretty women left for him in this world to look at because there were none more beautiful than Zainab, her mother, Noor, her sister, and she. The memory instantly brought tears to her eyes and those intimidating goons Depression and Loneliness simply vanished from her life leaving her happy in that moment there.

Keenie bhai offered her piping hot chicken Momo with chilly chutney. Momo perfectly gelled in the cold of that high-altitude morning. Even if they didn't, Momo was her favourite dish and an integral part of all menus of their family only because Shibra loved them. Many a time, Momo didn't fit the flavours of the food, but they were there for her. Shibra felt a sudden ache for her home – the safe place where she can go as she is and not be questioned. Living away from her home for a long time now, she suddenly realised that home is not a place, it's a feeling.

While Shibra picked up another Momo from the plate, Nuvem pointed out that the plate was broken on the side.

Shibra was in her element oozing charm lavishly, she looked at him and sprinkled some wit to say, "I think broken things have such a sad beauty. After years of stories and triumph and tragedy infused into them, they can be much more romantical than new things that haven't lived at all."

Nuvem smiled, such deeper lines from young Shibra, spoken so playfully, pleasantly surprised him. Though those words reflected her pain amply, they carried in them a semblance of her willingness to get past the gloom of yesterday morning's unsavoury episode. Opening up to her, he retorted, "What doesn't kill you gives you a set of unhealthy coping mechanisms and a dark sense of humour."

As Keenie quickly replaced the broken plate, Nuvem continued, "Remember Shibra, sad is never beautiful. Recently, I had been to the New Delhi World Book Fair at Pragati Maidan. You may be surprised but self-help books accounted for eighty percent of all books placed there. That goes on to show a very high level of unhappiness in our society, especially the educated and successful. Interestingly, such self-help stuff doesn't help without action and discipline. One has to do it herself or himself as the case may be. Action is the greatest wisdom."

"Who's self?"

"It's your conscience keeper. It has no power to directly make a difference. Even God won't do it for us. We have to do it ourselves and then only God helps. Haven't you heard an old saying – God helps those who help themselves."

Shibra looked at him in disbelief, her facial expressions were like what, God doesn't do it for us? Nuvem understood the enigma of her broken belief and said, "Let me tell you a story - when a little girl was in some trouble and she sought God's intervention. And God was very busy solving the problems of humans, but He actually came, and here's what transpired between the little girl and God.

What God said will open your eyes … God said, "Let me ask you something. If someone prays for patience, do you think God gives them patience? Or does he give them the opportunity to be patient? If they pray for courage, does God give them courage, or does he give them opportunities to be courageous? If someone prayed for their family to be closer, do you think God zaps them with warm, fuzzy feelings? Or does He give them opportunities to love each other?"

The little girl gasps quietly.

God finally says, "Well, I got to run. A lot of people to serve. Enjoy."

Nuvem continued, "God has entrusted us to ourselves to reiterate that we have a great strength hidden within. Look no further for help. Help yourself. Don't try to change things you cannot change, instead remove yourself away from things you cannot accept."

Shibra realised that Self can only suggest a method in the madness, but it's she who got to do and come out of sadness. Is sadness a place? Yes, sometimes people live there for years. She has been there for almost three years now. Deep grief sometimes is almost like a specific location, a coordinate on a map of time. When you are standing in that forest of sorrow, you cannot imagine that you can ever find your way to a better place. She had to understand that to be human is to track her way through this haunted forest in that unique expedition that she calls her life.

But if someone can assure you that they themselves have stood in that same place, and now they have moved on, sometimes this brings hope. Shibra believed that Nuvem was someone who could bring hope to her because he had managed to extricate himself from the forest of sorrow and moved on. But has he moved on? Really!!

She probed, "You didn't ask me anything about what was I up to in the morning yesterday on that road barrier on the road bend?"

"I didn't ask because I know you are going through a very difficult time in your life. I also understand you won't be able to explain your deadly indiscretion at that road bend. I am sure your pre-dawn compulsion or misadventure whatever you can call that was not the first and it won't be the last unless you shove away troubles from your charming life. So, rather than asking you the same depressing questions, we rather talk about what we can do to reach some sensible levels of sanity.

You see child, our case is almost identical. You lost your dad who was the pillar of strength for you, and I lost Vrishti who was the entire length and breadth of my life. I love my daughters and your mom loves you."

Shibra almost protested like a child, "No, I love her too."

"I know you surely do, but does she know you still love her? I mean for some time now you haven't made her feel that way. All you have done is focus on your pain and not her. Always remember like the loss of a parent, the loss of a spouse is a huge loss. She has lost her companion of life. And her heart must be breaking seeing you living like a nomad. Look at where your beautiful family is standing today, Dad has gone and mom and daughters are separated to fend for themselves, and you are living so dangerously. It's that obvious and yet it is not. Make a U-turn Shibra, you both need each other more than your mobile phones.

We love our digital devices more than our family and friends. They lead us into a virtual metaverse which seems like a delusionality of perfection. But that's a trap that separates us from our beautiful stories of the universe. They take us away from our loved ones. These digital devices are our worst enemies. They sell sadness on payment and additionally barter our time, tears, and peace of mind. You and I are a willing victim of the Sadness Economy. Grief, pain, and getting dumped are a very productive business model today on reels, feeds, and stories. The Tortured Poets Department of Taylor Swift is inspiring singers across the board to lend their mesmerising voices to dish out unhappy lyrics to sell sorrow and popularise pain and tears. These singers and poets inspire an Army of crying dolls who inundate and saturate Facebook and Instagram to post emotional stuff to spread sadness 24x7. Fake posts of Sufism mainly attributed to Jalal-u-Din Rumi only worsen the emotional environment of our minds.

You and I are a part of a significant section of our societies where our minds have turned against us. Thus, we are vulnerable, susceptible, and willing customers who are ever ready to fall prey to the frauds of the markets of emotions. We are happy to buy a lot of troubles and pain from a virtual world and claim its ownership in our stories of life. We fall in love with our pain and love tears in our eyes because that way we are conned into believing in our love for our loved ones who have gone. We forget that those for whom we cry loved us and as such they won't be happy seeing us in so much pain and sorrow because of them. Therefore, the least we can do is to remember them with a smile and celebrate our love for them. And those of us who have been left to live alone must love ourselves much more because they live in us. Crying is a worthless crime.

Remember sunshine is delicious, rain is refreshing, wind braces us up, snow is exhilarating; there is really no such thing as bad weather. We must live wisely. Living wisely includes living happily and at times dangerously when needed. Sometimes it also includes living unreasonably. In life, there are moments when you don't have to live dangerously, and at those moments rejoice and be content with the moment. One has to learn the art of balancing happiness and the rest in a proportion of ninety to ten percent.

There will be moments where you have to push yourself beyond your limits, and at that moment you have to live dangerously, meaning you put yourself at risk. Why do you say that we have to go beyond our limits? Our diffident mind creates certain limits, and we get limited by them. Be cautious of this fact. When we have poor self-esteem, then we set poor goals that appear reasonable. These limits imprison us.

Hence, there is an expression, 'Learn to be unreasonable'. This means going beyond the limits of your reason that has been polluted by poor self-esteem. All powerful people are unreasonable – not that they are unintelligent, but they are the ones who go beyond the limits of a diffident mind.

We should be neither be past-oriented, nor future-oriented, nor even present-oriented. We should have a balance of the past, present, and future, but live in the present.

The heaviest burden crushes us, we sink beneath it, and it pins us to the ground. But in love poetry of every age, the woman longs to be weighed down by the man's body. The heaviest of the burden is therefore simultaneously an image of life's most intense fulfilment. The heavier the burden, the closer our life comes to the earth, and the more real and truthful we become. Conversely, the absolute absence of burden causes man to be lighter than air, to soar into heights, take leave of the earth and his earthly being, and become only half real, his movements as free as they are insignificant. What shall we choose? Weight or lightness?

Lost Boy and the Pink Past

"Quantum Leap – What if I told you that the reason why you want certain things so deeply is because it's already yours at some point on the timeline? Your future self is whispering to you through intuitive feelings, dreams planted within, and crystal-clear vision. Those desires are not just wants; they're previews of what's already yours on the timeline of your life. Embody them in this present moment, for they are the breadcrumbs leading you to the manifestation of your destiny."

Nuvem looked at Shibra and said, "Whether you choose weight or lightness of your life, action will be the essence to take you through the pits and peaks. Life flows and for that reason, inertia will always be temporary. The crux lies in finding the flow once again albeit in an unknown normal. I am not sure what to choose, burden or lightness. Fortunately, I didn't have to choose anything because I was weighed down by life. Sometimes I wonder whether I have weathered the storm and healed. I feel I am fine, but not okay. The irony of my pain is that I want to be comforted by Vrishti who is no more.

Vrishti thought I was very strong and even I believed I was emotionally sorted. But that was one assumption of hers and mine that went horribly wrong after her demise. Her going away exposed me as an emotional sissy. I buckled up in emotions and lost my will to live. That was the lowest phase of my life and I had to measure up to a massive task of restoring the confidence of my beautiful residual family in themselves and me.

I was dragged into a new chapter that day when Vrishti suddenly chose to go. One that started when her life ended. I grabbed at the previous pages but life ripped them away. New chapters have come since and many of them are good. But I still find myself wanting to go back. To stay with her bookmarked in part of my life where she is still living.

My happiness resides in that part of my life where Vrishti lives. But the stark reality was that my entire universe came crashing down like a pack of cards immediately after she went and within three months of her passing away, I forfeited my will to survive. Her demise changed every single thing in my world going forward. The way I ate changed. The way I watched TV changed. My friend circle changed. My family dynamics changed. It affected my self-worth, my self-esteem, my confidence, and my rhythms.

I had the most expensive smile when she was alive and the first thing that happened within a short time of her going away was that my smile deserted me. I slipped into depression, developed very high blood pressure and sugar, and forgot to smile. I simply buckled up and went on my knees in the face of a major crisis for our beautiful family.

The loss of Vrishti severely affected peace of my mind. I was going through a terrible phase of my life. I had bouts of severe depression and I was getting disoriented. And I realised it when I went completely blank twice while driving my car and losing the way on the road that I frequently travelled.

I had issues with life. And so, I had her issues and daughters' issues. And maybe, I thought about death. Maybe, I don't understand the logic of the world. Maybe, I wonder about the world, how did we get here, and who are we. Maybe, I wonder about love. And the power of it. Why is death so strong and love so frail, and yet it's the strongest force on the planet?

My daughters are very strong. Vrishti and I brought them up like cubs. Unfortunately, they too were grappling with the loss of their mother and the wilting will of their father was an additional emotional burden on them. That dented their confidence levels in themselves and me hugely. Mercifully, our comfort levels with each other remained restored. That was a good rallying point for us to accept the new normal in our lives.

But that was not so easy because, like their father, they too were reeling under a massive emotional turmoil in their lives. The way they reacted to their respective grief was very different, yet they were both equally heartbroken.

Our elder one was fighting hard to come to terms with the loss of her mother who was the very basis of her life and her go-to Goddess. The sudden loss of her mother shattered her emotional support system. That hit her very hard and she lost the compass, focus, and fulcrum of her life. She became like a rudderless boat being tossed away by the mighty waves of a storm in the rough waters of an unfriendly ocean. She would get hallucinations in the middle of the night and cry uncontrollably. Her loving husband stood as a very strong pillar of her support. And though he was commanding an Army unit in a very difficult area in the face of the enemy, his support for her was unwavering.

My younger one was the worst hit. Initially, she decided to take control of the erring situation. She would slog the whole week in the office in New Delhi and then rush to be with me every weekend in Jaipur for almost three months after Vrishti. But she was not well and soon severe depression gripped her and she was fighting the dark thoughts. The young woman had taken a lot on herself. And she hid behind her work. She had to be persuaded to go on antidepressants. Her husband stood solid with her, but she folded into herself.

One day, glancing through Vrishti's WhatsApp messages, I came across the 'musings of a broken heart' of our younger daughter. She wrote those on 13th March 2024, her birthday. Her words sketched the happiness of our home when Vrishti was around. That was a grim reminder of a life left behind. That was also a wake-up call to re-kindle our bonds of love and rebuild our lives in the new normal.

Those musings of 13th March 2024 brought a stream of tears to my eyes. I was wondering why were my tears not drying, perhaps my sadness was balancing my feelings of happiness of the past. Getting back to the old business of bliss was not easy, many old markers of our happiness had to be unravelled and redefined once again, and the process had to go through plenty of care, affection, and lots of love. The value of life had to be carefully nurtured through patience and I realised that some valuable lessons of life were to be re-learnt mindfully and diligently.

The direction and the pathway were to be recognised and reconstructed. I didn't know how but the honesty of my thoughts cracked that riddle through the realisation that the pathway to the new normal of our lives lay in compassion, understanding, and the necessity of mutual emotional dependence. The process and sincerity of our efforts bore fruits and led us on a sacred path to bridge the gap between our old and new lives. The task was massive and implementation even more difficult. I took on the responsibility where failure couldn't be an option.

When I concentrated on my daughters, initially they were quite apprehensive and reluctant to acknowledge my outreach as their reliable support. Vrishti was the spine of our family. She was a fantastic woman of substance. No nonsense, but an able anchor of support and competent rudder guiding our lives into the safety of love. She mothered me along with my daughters. I accepted I would never be able to match her strengths, so I decided to find my own, a herculean task though.

I was a happy-go-lucky guy, a good man of good times who loved to spoil our daughters especially the younger one who was born eight years after our first-born. I could never discriminate, but admittedly, I was more inclined towards the younger one because she was a photocopy of her beautiful mom and more importantly, I was more mature, and comparatively free when she was born. I made wonderful materialistic connections with both of them, but Vrishti made those of the heart.

So, I had to play to the tunes of their sacred emotions. But for that, I had to discipline my own emotions which had run amok. That was a wake-up call and I had no option but to assume responsibility and take control of my life. It was then that I decided to work on my mental health and get things sorted in my mind. I started walking, trekking, and travelling to try and get my mind back on track.

In my Army career, I had been trained to do difficult things immediately and impossible things in little time. I had to recall all the robustness of my mind, replay them in my mind again and again, and yet again, and get on with the task at hand. I had to regain the trust of my daughters and expose them to the very same strength of mine that had stood by them throughout their charmed lives.

I had decided to confront reality up front and get going. I began by healing my relationship with them and myself. I had accepted that I could never be the mother to them. No father can mother children because mothers are special gifts of God to all lives in the Universe. In my case, I even forgot to be the father to them after they lost their mother.

I walked the talk of my mind and reached out to my children with the confidence that as a father I could take care of them to a point where they overcame the setback and took control of their lives more gracefully. I was all along a caring and sensitive father and that helped rebuild the cracking balustrades of trust amongst all of us. I had to believe in my strengths, those very strengths that formed an invisible bond on the basis of which external connections emerged among us. The fact that every father is the first love of his daughters had to emerge and come to the fore or so I sincerely believed. That would happen only when the external connections seamlessly transformed into formidable inner connections. The honesty of love is the key because external and internal connections are not mutually exclusive.

I had to make changes in me. The first change that came in handy was that I started listening to them patiently without dishing out instant solutions for their every problem. That was difficult but I disciplined myself to stick to patience. I found serendipity to the extent that I understood how important it was to just listen to women!! Not that I didn't judge them but I stopped pronouncing the judgements. I had learned that excess of knowledge would always be injurious to love and that love will always be stronger than knowledge. I had to learn that if there was a conflict between emotion and logic, I had to let emotions win. The mission was to help them heal themselves and more importantly, heal myself through a process of honesty.

The other thing that I did was to put in place a very rudimentary, but effective administrative apparatus that assured them that their home was still the best and most secure place for them. I did everything possible to keep the home exactly the way Vrishti kept it. Externally, our home is beautiful, but internally it still lacks the dynamics and vibrancy of Vrishti. The affection of Vrishti's home reached my daughters and my sisters and they were rest assured that their Maika (Mother's home) was welcoming though not as comfortable as it was when Vrishti was around. And most importantly, we as a family found each other, invisible bonds amongst us resurfaced and became ever stronger. The bonds rebuilt in mutual pain and adversities are the strongest.

My daughters have got on with their loves and lives. I don't interfere with their lives, but they always find me when they need me. I am no longer lonely. I have upgraded myself to be alone. Vrishti lives in me. I cannot imagine life minus Vrishti. She stays in my heart because that is the reason I stay happy. But I had to take baby steps towards solitude for further firming in my relationship with her, my family, and myself.

On a scale of ten, I give myself five for my healing. That makes me somewhat composed externally, but sporadic battles rage within. Life is a guiding force and a score of five is good given my quest is only to reach a score of eight which would be enough for me to live on and maybe love on. Life minus Vrishti is more skewed and I will be happy pursuing that added imperfection for the rest of my life.

The idea of life is abstract. Loving life doesn't mean you love life itself. You love places, animals, people, memories, food, literature, and music, and sometimes you meet someone who requires all the love you have to give. If you lose that someone, you think everything else will stop too but everything just keeps on going. But whether you love life or not, life stands by you through your crises and it longs for the same love that you gave her before you met that someone. And life knows your perfect score on a scale of ten is eight and not ten but she won't accept anything less than ten. And that's because life makes you love her even more."

Travel Into Unknown Terrain

"Aut Viam Inveniam Aut Faciam – I shall either find a way or make one."

Shibra was listening intently to Nuvem's story and trying to relate it to her status of being in a constant state of flux. She wondered why her standpoint was so different from Nuvem's outlook on life given the equal amount of time they had travelled since the loss of their loved ones. The possible explanation perhaps was their natures were different and hence their responses to the same stimuli varied. More importantly, Nuvem was trying to break free and Shibra somehow remained chained to her circumstances. She was like a shining black stallion whose reins were thrown loosely around a plastic chair placed in the middle of a huge ground, and the mighty horse thought it was impossible to break free. It was indeed a reality of stupidity.

However, having heard his story she couldn't consider him emotionally any stronger than her and that was an encouraging empowerment. An empowerment of being as weak as the other! She instantly smiled at the folly of feeling good with the knowledge that the person sitting in front of her was equally miserable. Immediately a question crossed her mind what motivated Nuvem to assume control of his life? Perhaps, the love he had for his daughters! All that she had to do was to keep her mother in focus and outwit her mind.

However, she was unable to fathom the trigger that would grant her access to such a sanity in her life. Unable to subdue her curiosity, she asked, "So you are saying time is a healer and feelings are normalised with time, maybe, the duration can vary depending upon individual mental makeups?"

Nuvem did understand the context and he replied, "Yes, time is certainly a healer to the extent it makes you feel you have traversed further from your black swan event and the distance reduces the intensity and frequency of pain. However, time plays hardly any role in changing your status as a human being whose grief has intensified his or her love for someone she or he loved and lost. Time only takes you far into the Disneyland of unknown and uncertain territory to charter a course for you with or without your consent and gives you the hope of a better deal to soothe your battered life. I am fragile, and so is everyone. Crust has formed, inside is hot molten lava!" Accept, realise, and keep trying to find happiness in actualising the Disneyland within.

Shibra tried to intervene but Nuvem gestured for her to hold on for a while and went in his flow, "I am an Infantryman, and I have been taught that mind is the master, body has to obey its command, and physical pain is a potent antidote to the mental suffering. Army makes you travel and travel a lot to different places. The postings in far-flung remote places, in inhospitable terrains, and extremely hostile climatic conditions are sometimes life-threatening but always transformative. Some of these places are virgin, hardly ever visited by humans for sheer difficulty of survival. Such places are breathtakingly beautiful and restorative.

But concerns of survival, unfortunately, render conscious viewing of amazing nature in those wonderful lands impossible. And at younger ages, life plays to invigorating tunes to fill hope of a brighter future in your dreamy eyes and that blocks the then unwanted deeper view of one's life. That's why younger guys and girls are prettier, stronger, happier, and internally much lighter.

Having said that, I must acknowledge that those fortunate youngsters who have been baptised by the rigours of Army life, imbibe and hold the reserves of fortitude and strength, unknowingly though, that come to the fore when confronted with the challenges of life at any age. Travel transforms and shapes their perspectives and outlooks on life permanently.

After I retired from the Army, there was a lull in our lives. We travelled but travel frequency was regularly irregular. We had to give time to our daughters to grow wings and fly into their future. Once our daughters were settled, we wanted to travel together extensively once again and we bought a Sports Utility Vehicle (SUV) accordingly. Unfortunately, she fell ill exactly seven days after the purchase; never to recover. After some time, when I regained a bit of my composure, I began solo travelling and accessed the benevolence of travel serendipity – solitude serendipity, the serendipity of getting lost, happiness, and eventually some semblances of hiraeth."

Shibra was intrigued as to why her wandering was not yielding the desired peace in her life. She felt she was missing out on something important. She asked, "Is travelling or more appropriately wandering, as my dad would call it, key to getting you back to what you were before tragedy struck you?"

"I would say yes and further qualify it to add that it makes you even better, broken but beautiful. But you will never be the same."

"Why and how?"

"Ours is not to question why, but to do, flow, and fly. Why, I don't know, but how, I will tell you. You see breathing is both a science and art of reaching within and the only method that makes meditation and spirituality accessible and nobody knows why. But that's not important. What is important is that we can learn to breathe. Similarly, travelling is transformative and it is a matter of education by experience. We don't know why is travelling transformative but we have to step out of our comfort zones, travel far and wide, and transform."

"Okay, tell me how?"

Nuvem smiled at her desperation to cling to something or someone who would show her the way to liberate her from the prison of her thoughts. Shibra was a loveable child and Nuvem felt her sufferings and anxieties were attracting his growing affection for her. It wasn't pity but empathy in its purest form. She felt comfortable with the way Nuvem was looking at her and she simply asked, "Coffee?"

Nuvem desperately needed one and before he could say that, Shibra had already poured coffee for him. Recognition and fulfillment of an unstated need is always an act of love and to that extent, it is always very gratifying. They sipped hot coffee quietly and it was refreshing. Shibra was waiting for his answer to her question, he knew it and said, "I am very fond of a Mark Twain's quote on the merits of travel that said, 'Travel is fatal to prejudice, bigotry, and narrow-mindedness, and many of our people need it sorely on these accounts. Broad, wholesome, charitable views of things cannot be acquired by vegetating in one little corner of the earth all one's lifetime.' This is a very powerful and sensible statement on life and it became the mantra for my physics of the quest. It also meant that we can't be living the same year 75 times and call it life. Shibra, how of everything lies in action, and only action. You have to learn to breathe, step out of your comfort zone, let life flow unbridled, and peace will welcome you with open arms.

So, what does travel do to us? Do we come back home as a different person? Travel could be a spiritual experience that shakes off our usual certainties and connects us to a richer, vaster world. When we are in a new place, we can't define ourselves as we used to be. We must seek out places that overturn our assumptions and so our quest will send us back as a different person than the one who left home. Travel humbles and releases us, and presents to us a new realisable reality.

All of us may not have an intensely transformative experience but, certainly, there are several positive benefits of travel, of getting out of our comfort zone and experiencing new people, cultures, and geographies. When we are safe at home, we think we know what we need to know – until we step into the wider world.

We get to see the intersection of cultures and faiths, traditions and languages. Curiously, many places of pilgrimage like Kedar Nath, Badri Nath, or Hem Kund Sahib are also places of unmatched beauty and very few would come out from there being unmoved towards solutions and hope for peace in the spirit of surrender and love.

If you read ancient scriptures, you will find our sages and monks kept travelling mostly to difficult terrains in search of the truth and they have come out with amazing insights and pearls of wisdom which are universally relevant. I wanted to wander in search of a miracle that would slow down my mind and I stepped out of my comfort spaces."

"You mean you unknowingly became a de facto Novaturient Solivagant?"

"Travel connects, travel unites, travel liberates. That way, all of us are Novaturient Solivagants and it is truer for life. While many people embark on their journey with companions, a special enchantment arises when we opt for or are forced to travel alone. The purpose is to dance with independence, a yearning for transitory belonging, and a discovery of self-amidst the unexpected. "Kabhi Kabhi Dur Tak Bikhre Hue Kuch Nahi Mein Khud Se MulaKaat Ho Jati Hai." (Sometimes in the middle of nowhere we find ourselves.)

Personally, I have always wanted to travel alone and see the world through a different lens and fortunately for me, there was no dread of vulnerability in my loneliness though it gave out constant reminders of its existence. I discovered that travelling alone was all about me! Choosing where to go, what to do, when to eat my favorite continental food that I first tasted at NDA, no hassles, just total freedom, the freedom I was not even sure whether I wanted it. But it enabled me to pursue myself.

Every turn provides an opportunity to meet the most extraordinary people. I realise that being on your own might be frightening at first; it requires strength and lots of courage, but you always emerge stronger and a better version of yourself in the end. It provides you with a once-in-a-lifetime opportunity to finally listen to yourself, appreciate your own company, and discover what your heart truly desires. It's like hugging yourself and being your own best friend.

At times you may feel lonely. The feeling is similar to unexpected rain on a picnic day. The excitement is not completely lost, but there's a wet cold that takes the edge off. You may find yourself surrounded by beautiful landscapes yet yearning for a peal of shared laughter beneath the stars. The emotion is real, it exists, and it must exist because of the absence of someone who loved you and whom you still love.

I accepted the fact that this feeling will always be there. The only way to deal with this feeling is to accept it completely. I must accept my independence and remember I have complete freedom to do whatever I choose! Whenever loneliness longed for my company during the journey, I used this freedom to get rid of it. I would ditch the itinerary and march out to explore the eerie secret in hidden alleys and indulge in the extra helping of my favourite food. This newfound freedom may be thrilling, reminding me that I am capable and powerful.

Even if it seems to be a horrible thing, keep in mind that loneliness does not always have to be a bad thing, quite an oxymoron though. Make the most of it by connecting with yourself. Read a book, note down your thoughts, or simply lie down and listen to your favourite music while allowing the actual world to be your genuine travel companion. These quiet times may be incredibly insightful and fulfilling. And then it happens.

One day you wake up and you're in this place where everything feels right, your heart is calm, your soul is lit, and your thoughts are positive. At peace with where you've been, at peace with what you've been. And at peace with where you're headed. The peace is not permanent, but it lingers to grant an ability to face your problem elegantly.

Towards the end of my journey, these unknown lands become my second home. I realise that home is not a physical four-wall structure that surrounds me, but rather an emotion. The warmth of shared laughter reverberating in a tangy pub, the quiet company of a sunrise shared with fellow travellers, and the kindness of people assisting me when I am walking like a dead zombie are the blessings of the unknown lands. Such moments give me a sense of belonging in strange lands, and I only have this because I have learnt how to deal with the painful sensation of loneliness. I can confidently state that after all these ups and downs, I have evolved into a better version of myself, Nuvem Mark II.

Having travelled extensively during my active service I had some sacred experiences in the mountains and jungles of both Arunachal Pradesh and Nagaland. I neither knew nor nurtured nor sought divine experiences. These were bestowed upon me through the fear of the unknown when I was pushed onto the thin line separating death from life. In those very special moments, I felt feather-light without fear and floating in the blessings of the supreme soul. The feeling was real and it was beyond the power of the words to capture. After all, words are only a frequency, and that too is different for different times!

Unfortunately, the experience would be a forgotten moment I was assured of being alive. I mentioned this to you to tell you that post-Vrishti my physics of the quest had picked up travelling in a graduated manner to seek the illusive sacred experiences which I desperately needed to tide over my troubles and flip my perspective. So, I motivated myself to step out of my comfort zone to travel first to exotic locations purely for pleasure.

The aim was to enjoy the colours of the petals of a beautiful flower with an ultimate aim to experience the source of its fragrance with the hope to chance upon the illusive peace beyond pleasure. My experience of the Northeast of India beckoned me to look for it by upgrading my pleasure to peace in a sojourn through the forests and mountains."

"Let's go on the spur right across."

"Done."

SPENDING TIME IN A FOREST

"Whose woods these are I think I know. His house is in the village though; He will not see me stopping here to watch his woods fill up with snow ... The woods are lovely, dark, and deep ..."

– Excerpts of the poem of Robert Frost

After breakfast, Nuvem and Shibra went trekking on Fagu Spur. The ascent was gradual, Nuvem's pace was rhythmic and slow, but he was encountering breathlessness because of falling oxygen levels at a higher altitude. Finally, after about one hour they reached the top. The view from the top was amazing. Clouds hid the mountains and beyond mountains there were higher mountains, and in higher mountains was Mount Kailash which could not be seen from Fagu.

But the awareness of the presence of Kailash Parbat somewhere in those mountains, initiated prayers and cosplay vibes in both Shibra and Nuvem and they felt energised. As long as one feels the energies of nature, reasons must become insignificant. Their entire outlook became positive and they had a beautiful panoramic view of the scenic landscapes of Fagu and Kufri spread out for them. The valley had apple orchards and the apple trees were covered in shade nets to prevent fruit sunburn and protect trees against hail damage.

Once they settled down comfortably, Shibra wanted Nuvem to carry on with his story of travel serendipity. He continued from where he left, "Remember Shibra, all travels begin for fun. You wish to indulge, eat the choicest of foods, drink to your heart, and generally dive into pleasure. The thought of good times initiates journeys that for some become addictive. This is what I call a positive addiction and it is potentially transformative in the end.

I too wandered for the lure of pleasure. In my case, pleasure had a motive too. I began travelling in order to disrupt the patterns of my destructive and poisonous thought process. When I realised that, the only question at hand was, "How do I define pleasure? How is pleasure most efficiently maximised?

And my loneliness had put me in a situation that would permit me to explore that question freely, and everything changed. Everything became … delicious including me. I became that cheeky human who never doubted his deliciousness since! All I had to do was to ask myself every day, for the first time in my life, "What would you enjoy doing today, Nuvem? What would bring you pleasure right now? With nobody else's agenda to consider and no other obligations to worry about, this question finally became distilled and absolutely self-specific.

It was interesting for me to discover what I did not want to do in places I was travelling to, once I'd given myself specific authorisation to enjoy my experience there. There are so many milestones of pleasure in places, and I did not have time to sample them all. You have to kind of declare a pleasure major there, or you'll get overwhelmed. That being the case I did not get into shopping, cinema, or museums. I didn't even want to look at art. I did, however, visit many monasteries and even trekked with one monk in Ladakh. I found all I wanted was to eat delicious food and experience the essence of the places. That was it. So, I declared a double major, really – in experiencing and eating (with a concentration on continental food).

The amount of pleasure this eating and experiencing brought to me was inestimable, and yet so simple. I passed so much time that might look like nothing much to the outside observer, but which I would always count amongst the happiest of my life. Until – as often happened during those first months of travel, whenever I would feel such happiness – my guilt alarm went off.

Vrishti would effortlessly walk into my thoughts and make my eyes misty, though she always came to keep the promise we made to travel together.

One obvious topic still needed to be addressed concerning my whole pursuit of pleasure thing in my life, "What about sex?" Or more appropriately, intimacy, and cosy companionship.

To answer that question simply, I didn't want to have any after she had gone.

Once that was settled, my life was simplified. My craving for good food and my fondness for the randomness of the pandemonium of life slowly eased me into longing for the solitude of forests and mountains. Arunachal Pradesh and Nagaland were far off and I was not even fit enough to traverse those terrains at my age.

So, I chose options closer to home. Fortunately, there are many small forests in my home town itself. Jhalana Forest is one of them and it is situated just three km away from where

I live. That's my favourite go-to forest for sheer convenience. Ranthambore and Sariska Tiger Reserves are located at a convenient distance from my hometown, Jaipur. And simpler mountains of Himachal Pradesh, Uttarakhand, and even Ladakh are easily accessible from Jaipur.

Whenever I can, I spend time in Smriti Van (Forest) which is an extension of Jhalana Forest and Panther Safari. Just about a week before I came to Fagu, I spent a lovely Sunday morning in the woods. When I was climbing a small spur, the music of the birds chirping only deepened the silence of the woods as I explored solitude in the forest. The weather was good and the clouds were happy to hold the rains. Suddenly, the music of the birds became shriller, the chattering of the peacocks got louder, and the calling of the blue-buck became bigger. I thought there was a panther around somewhere and I decided to backtrack. But neither the blue-bucks nor the peacocks left their respective locations thereby effectively ruling out the possibility of the presence of the panther. But then, the clouds roared from above, and I realised there was a tiger! Yes, a tiger who was scaring them. And that tiger was I! I am a scary fellow.

After spending some two hours in the calm serenity there, I decided to walk back home for a different hue of solitude. But poor cloud could no longer hold his rain, so she left him. But where could she go leaving her cloud alone? She came down only to find a parched Nuvem grounded to Mother Earth, waiting for her to return to him. She had put on weight in the happiness of her heavenly abode, she fell heavy on me, and I felt her subtle beingness.

I told her I thought you were rain that I was ready to soak in, but you became the hurricane that swept my home away. She was water-powerful enough to drown me, soft enough to cleanse me, and deep enough to save me."

Shibra was a bit confused but then she immediately realised Nuvem had swayed in his emotions. She said, "Poet Robert Frost wrote, "The woods are lovely, dark and deep. But I have promises to keep and miles to go before I sleep …"

That got Nuvem back on track, he smiled and continued, "To some others, however, forests are unknown terrain, scary places, so dark and deep and not-so-lovely. The fear of the unknown takes over, for forests are mysterious wonderlands or nightmares, depending on whose perspective it is. Forests are pregnant with so much life below the ground as there is above. And what if one gets lost? Texas-based mythologist Stephanie Zajchowski says that once, on her way to a cave in a Belizean forest, she fell behind her group as she was mesmerised by the lush surroundings and lost her way; her heart started racing with fear. She began recollecting stories that revealed how the forest could be both dangerous and transformative.

Adventures led heroines and heroes into the forest, and a few were left unchanged. Reuniting with her group eventually, Zajchowski discerned that one of the most valuable takeaways from that adventure was that she had begun to feel comfortable about being lost. Getting lost is an essential part of finding our way, she says. Because self-discovery outside the bounds of social constructs meant we were in uncharted territory, wandering, seeking, and finding until a path presented itself – as opposed to a path carved out by someone else.

For those who stay in an urban jungle for most of the year, a quick visit to a forest is always a pleasurable break. The best way to enjoy it is not to drive through a forest but to walk through it at different times of the day.

Walking through a forest or forest bathing is a sensory journey, and each step is a connection to a world teeming with life, from the tiniest insects to towering trees.

If one listens carefully and intently, one can hear several soundtracks, each unique. I have been fortunate enough to walk through the jungles (Forests) of both Nagaland and Arunachal Pradesh.

Nagaland was in the grips of insurgency and one had to be alert to traps and sudden attacks of the insurgents. So, walking through the jungles there was a very tedious, dangerous, and very stressful process. On the other hand, the jungles of Arunachal Pradesh were raw and virgin. The terrain and climatic conditions were very hostile. Walking through them was extremely difficult, dangerous, and life-threatening. Moreover, those jungles were heavily infested with pythons, snakes, and blood-guzzling leaches.

The common factor in the jungles of Nagaland and Arunachal Pradesh was fear of death. Intense concentration on the thoughts of death at any moment there enforced a meditative stance upon me and I discovered that the fear could be immensely therapeutical. My heartbeats would be so loud that they drowned the sounds of flowing blood in my veins. I could hear my heartbeats even amidst the sounds of the falling rain, flowing streams, and the strange noises of jungles. The happiness of coming out alive after every outing of duty in those jungles was no way any less than the bliss.

I had spent many scary nights in the forests of the North East and the only experience there was fear. Not only the fear of the unknown but real fear. I felt the intensity of the fear of the unknown was much lesser than the actual feeling of fear. And the only experience of fear was fear.

The experience will be different if one is lucky enough to spend a night in a forest in the knowledge of being safe and secure. In such a case, the sense of fear gives way to experiencing the essence and mysteries of forests. Our younger daughter, Vrishti, and I got an opportunity to spend one such night in a forest resthouse in the tiger reserve of Sariska.

While it took a bit of time to adjust to the calm environs, the new sounds, and the darkness, a new world opened in no time. The clear, starlit sky was the cherry on the cake. Though we were safe, the awareness of the presence of the tigers around us added to the mystery of the jungles and that was an exhilarating experience.

In the pre-dawn stillness, the forest underwent another transformation. The symphony of the night gradually gave way to the waking of early birds, announcing the imminent arrival of dawn. Witnessing the first light break through the canopy was a profound experience, a moment of serene beauty, and a testament to the resilient spirit of the forest. Forest bathing is indeed transformative and rejuvenating."

Love is All About Giving

"I think people really fall in love once for real. After that, they just roam the earth miserably looking for a similar version of their first love."

Nuvem was telling Shibra about the transformative powers of travelling and wandering to encourage her to come out of her comfort zone and offload her toxic thoughts into the magnanimity of mother nature. He had correctly assessed that she was being tormented by her depression and if she had to dump it, nature was the lap to lie.

Shibra was a youngster and the age difference between them was a differentiator in their outlook on life. Nuvem was in the contented phase of his life whereas Shibra was in the most productive phase of life, but she was still struggling with depression. Nuvem sincerely wished she overcome her condition soon and reclaim her charmed life, and he believed she was capable enough to do that and she would do it.

Shibra was still a stranger. That was a plus point in a manner that Nuvem could share his vulnerabilities with her without the fear of being judged. Nuvem found it quite comfortable to open up to her even on his intimacy issues irrespective of his age. Do older people still crave the intimacy of women?

He said, "Forests have certainly upgraded my pleasure issues, food cravings went down and I became more selective in my choices. At the same time, my quest for experience got upgraded. However, I had to contemplate my need for companionship and to answer it more thoroughly and honestly - of course, sometimes I do desperately want to have some, but I've decided to sit this particular game out for a while. I don't want to get involved with anybody. When I get lonely these days, I think; So, be lonely, Nuvem. Learn your way around loneliness. Make a map of it. Sit with it, for once in your life. Welcome to the human experience. But never again use another person's body or emotions as a scratching post for your own unfulfilled yearnings.

It's a kind of emergency lifesaving policy, more than anything else.

Moreover, I have boundary issues with women. Or maybe that's not fair to say. To have issues with boundaries, one must have boundaries in the first place, right? But I have disappeared into Vrishti who is the only woman I have loved. I am a permeable membrane. If I love you, you can have everything. You can have my time, my devotion, my money, my family, my passions, my commitments – everything. If I love you, I will carry for you all your pains, I will assume for you all your debts (in every definition of the word), I will protect you from your insecurity, I will project upon you all sorts of good qualities that you have never actually cultivated in yourself and I will buy gifts for you for almost no reasons. I gave Vrishti all this and more, and now I am so exhausted and depleted that I don't want to recover my energies anymore.

I do relay these facts about myself with pride because this is how it's always been with her. And I am lucky that she has taken all this with her. Now I have taken a break to give myself some space to discover what I look like when I'm not trying to merge with someone. And also, let's be honest – it might be a generous public service for me to leave intimacy alone for a while.

There's a final reason I'm hesitant to get involved with someone else. I still happen to be in love with her, and I don't think that's fair to the next lady. I must admit that I harbour no hopes that maybe someday I stumble upon them … maybe. I humbly accept that neither I am a doer nor reason, yet I am there in this world for some reason!

I don't know.

This much I do know – I am exhausted by the cumulative consequences of a lifetime of hasty choices, chaotic passions, and injured emotions. My body and my spirits are depleted. I feel like the soil on some desperate sharecropper's farm, sorely overworked and needing a fallow season. So that's why I quit, came out of my comfort zone, and proceeded to understand the physics of the quest and experiment with Mr. Mark Twain's take on travelling.

While walking back both of them were quiet. Nuvem wished Shibra to reunite with her mother asap and they pick up pieces of their lives and heal mutually. Shibra was also contemplating what Nuvem had spoken that afternoon. And she was a tad bit disappointed.

Shibra had nursed a secret desire of a possible companionship for her mother and she considered Nuvem to be a potential companion for her. However, hearing Nuvem's stance against any alliance nipped her desire in the bud. She knew it was a difficult wish because it sought an unlikely companionship of two aging elders who were committed to the memories of their respective spouses and devoted parents who had never met each other in their lives. But somehow, she was comfortable with her thought when even in the wildest of her dreams, she couldn't imagine any other man in her mother's life. She knew well that her mother too would never accept anyone else in her life, yet she wanted to give shape to that thought. That was because Nuvem was different. Desires don't rest because God is a magician who feeds reasons to authenticate the need for desires!

She had already constructed a relationship matrix for Nuvem and her mother in her mind that was hard to explain. It was a paradox of wanting and still not wanting!

Fully engrossed in those abstract thoughts she reached her room to steal a little nap. When she woke up, she thought of Nuvem's view on the power of travelling. Frankly, she was not convinced because she felt what Nuvem spoke was too theoretical and there was nothing experiential about travelling. Then she immediately corrected herself. Experiencing beyond obvious is a personal accomplishment that was yet to dawn in her life.

There was something very strange about the words because most of the time when spoken they lose their intended sense. This probably happens because more often than not words when spoken are covered in perceptional biases and are heard through the filters of experiences and social conditioning of the listener.

But Nuvem's words felt worthwhile because Shibra could see a possible path to her redemption. And to walk the path, she must behave responsibly, concentrate on their family business, and be a worthy daughter to her mother.

Her baby steps towards her life were surely shaping up in a new reality.

Eudaimonia – Human Flourishing

"You might preen at all your material achievements, but Nature puts you in your place. You are just a fragile human up against the mountains and the furry of the clouds. Nature is a great leveller. It makes you humble, more contemplative, more determined."

The next day they did not go out trekking, instead spent time in the cosy comforts of the sunroom. Shibra was in a pensive mood which Nuvem interpreted as she battling another bout of loneliness. Then suddenly she said, "You upgraded your pleasure by tuning into forests, but you still feel the pangs of your loneliness."

"Yes, but her memories every time they visit me, which they do all the time, don't torment me anymore. They make me feel better and don't leave me lonely. I have accepted them as a very good company for me. However, I have to move on and that means I have to reduce my emotional dependence on them to find more balance in my life.

Look at this beautiful flower. The outer life is like a beautiful flower … inner life its fragrance. If there is no fragrance, we cannot appreciate the flower, and if there is no flower, how can there be any fragrance? So, the inner life and the outer life must go together. Right now, our lives are a bit imbalanced because our inner lives are lagging behind our outer pretensions. The need here is to hit upon Eudaimonia and Peace.

The relentless chase for pleasure often leads to the 'hedonistic treadmill, a cycle where gratification is fleeting and the desire for more intensifies. This pursuit, centred around material possessions, offers only temporary satisfaction. However, eudaimonia emerges as a profound alternative beyond this superficial allure, leading to enduring contentment.

Eudaimonia, a Greek concept translated as human flourishing, signifies a life well-lived. It's about finding meaning, purpose, and virtue in one's existence. Unlike the indulgent focus on pleasure, eudaimonia emphasises spiritual growth and contributing to something larger than oneself.

Spiritual practices such as meditation, prayer, and mindfulness play a crucial role in cultivating eudaimonia. Spirituality empowers individuals to break free from the sybaritic cycle by shifting focus from external rewards to internal peace. It offers a resilient foundation for happiness that is less susceptible to the fluctuations of external circumstances. Research consistently demonstrates the positive correlation between spirituality and well-being.

Integrating the principles of eudaimonia encourages a life of virtue and meaningful fulfillment while understanding the sensual treadmill helps balance the pursuit of transient pleasures. Together with spiritual practices, it fosters lasting inner peace."

"And how would it happen?"

"I really don't know how but a touch of nature offers the way. I am an Infantryman. Army repeatedly put me into nature and the young boy in me was transformed into being the soldier who had mastered the ground and the art of darkness. That was a tactical transformation, but it was indeed a great transformation. How and why of it I never knew and never questioned. But I knew I had to go back to nature to upgrade and internalise my pleasure to the highest levels possible within my capability as a normal human being.

When I went there again, an inner voice said – Look at Nature – the lyricism of petals, and the joy of trees in giving, and the music of birds. Nature does have a soul. It lives in the rhythm of creation. Rain falls during the season, but the grace of the God Almighty pours all the time. Experience the spirit of the season and the rhythm of nature for they form the rhythm of life, which is a joy in itself.

The cycle and rhythm of nature are indeed very invigorating and rejuvenating. When the rhythm of nature is in sync with the rhythm of our breathing, we discover that we are deeply connected with the universe through nature. Being linked with nature brings joy and peace as this is an acknowledgement of the secret laws of the universe. Two things bring rhythm into life – slow pace and meditative silence. Adopt the pace of nature. Her secret is patience.

High mountains are the home to many of the happiest places in the world. The happitude and quietude of mountains give a glimpse of the magnitude of the power of nature. The happy places stand still with time, where everything seems to be right out of a magical painting. It's a region where the journey itself is a destination. It's both tranquil and adventurous with stunning sights to behold. It's fulfilling because it lets you explore not only what is outside but also what is within – your mettle and your matter.

Go to great mountains, and if you are fortunate, you will be privileged to meet there with the spirits of the winds and pleasure to see fluted snow ridges and snow-spume blown like smoke into trailing banner clouds.

You will be able to feel the awful presence of creative forces and wonder at the beauty and power of nature. See a sunrise and a sunset, a moonrise, and moonset, and then be at peace with yourself. This is the stuff of internalisation. There are many places in the North-East of India where nature is undisturbed and virgin. Imagine no humans, only high mountains, densest of vegetation, tall trees touching the clouds, birds, reptiles, pythons, unperturbed wildlife, the flowing streams of water churning as white as milk, and where the sounds of flowing water and blowing winds compose a soothing and melodious music of nature. The sounds and voices of nature only deepen your silence.

I have been blessed to travel to Jorging which lies beyond Miging where back in time the last human habitation ended in Siang Valley in Arunachal Pradesh. It took five days of a tough trek along the jungle trails to reach Jorging from Miging which was the last village of human inhabitation on that route. That was the toughest trek I have done in my life. Similarly, in the Siyom Valley of Arunachal Pradesh ahead of Mechuka and Manigong, there are places like Lamang, Tadadege, and Yarlung where there was no human habitation a long time back when I served in those areas. These were the places where the distinctions between external and internal were obliterated and my mind opened up spaces to allow me to reach myself. This is what nature is all about. This is bliss.

I have travelled over Assam, Arunachal Pradesh, and Nagaland extensively. The enigmatic land beyond the Brahmaputra is rich in rapturous beauty, cultural diversity, and spiritual serenity. The fresh mountain air in the Eastern Himalayas is fragrant and filled with so much joy. Music reverberates in the hills, be it the harmony of Church choirs or the traditional beats unique to each tribe. Hills, forests, and rivers are sacred in tribal life. This is why two-thirds of its land remains under forest cover. Life is rooted in local – village, clan, and community are the first markers of tribal identity.

Having had an intimate experience of pure nature in those inaccessible and virgin areas, I had no desire to travel after I left the Army. But circumstances of my life compelled me to travel as a survival instinct post the demise of Vrishti. But I was not fit enough to access those places again. So, I zeroed in on Ladakh which was tough but accessible.

I would describe Ladakh as being the same as Arunachal Pradesh and Nagaland sans the trees and vegetation attire. It's a bald and extremely cold beauty of nature where ultraviolet rays of sun burn you. Actually, there are some things that cannot be put into words, Love is one of them and then there is Ladakh – the land of scenic beauty, rustic charm, and nature at its best. Whenever I tried to recollect Ladakh, it was always about losing myself in those brilliant moments spent in the lap of the majestic Himalayas.

My first visit to Ladakh was mostly fun-oriented but I carried back some unknown vibes that still reverberate in me. This time around I had to find the meaning of those vibes solely as a survival attribute of my life after Vrishti. I was looking for an impossible quest even beyond my imagination. And then there was a scent of spirituality in the rarer air of Ladakh. Solely on those counts, I had to learn and experience conscious viewing beyond the obvious. That was not going to be easy. But there was hope because newer perspectives resided in a higher degree of difficulty. Duly armed with such abstractions, I nursed the ambition of getting lost, yes, getting lost yet again!

I feel that's a privilege because being comfortable in getting lost is a special blessing that graces only a few lives. I am convinced that getting lost is about finding ways because self-discovery resides in uncharted territory, wandering, seeking, and finding until a path presents itself. At times, there's an inspiring feeling like, "Aut Viam Inveniam Aut Faciam." (Either I will find a way or make one.)

Solitude offers a kind of spontaneity that is a fine art and a celebration of getting lost. It's a memorable moment that results from a fortuitous misstep. After all, sometimes the best way to find your feet in a new place is to get well and truly lost. I wanted to experience and understand my meaning of getting lost. I wanted to experience what Texas-based mythologist Stephanie Zajchowski felt when she was lost in the cave of the Belizean forest. When you reach nowhere, you are suddenly hit by the beauty around you and you well up with tears. In such special moments, you access your vantage spot from where life is about absorbing and appreciating your immediate surroundings, and not caring whether a story about them would impress anyone."

And the Mountains Echoed

"Julley! (Namaste)

Heart of stone and a wild soul, I invite you to walk through the valleys of my heart. It's a maze of nothingness, guarded by the mighty mountains of sand and stone raised by my mind that guard against the incursions of the likes of you.

The winding smooth roads and the incredible views entice you to delve deeper ... the barren brown tunnel that lures you deeper and deeper towards clear blue skies and starry nights.

You stand in the middle of nowhere, washed by the harsh sun and cold gushes of the wind, mesmerised by the unparalleled beauty of my raw nature, unaware that I am going to take your breath away, leaving you parched and I will make your heart beat faster than it ever has. As the day comes to a close, I shall inhabit you as the chill in your bones ...

You find me ruthless, harsh, unforgiving, dead, and a threat to your mundane way of life ... a cold barren desert.

But do you see the life pulsing through my veins ... the ice-cold turquoise flow of Indus, Shyok, and Zanskar meandering amidst a sea of my grey and brown mindscape? Or is it simply a picturesque background for your next Instagram post?

You were right when you said that I was incapable of being loved for more than a week or maybe a fortnight ... because it takes patience, perseverance, and fortitude to love someone like me.

I can stand unwavered in the scorching heat of the sun and against the unbridled force of the cold winds ... I can wear a crown of snow every night amassed after a day of hard-earned labour and see it melt away with first light every morning, proudly displaying the scars left behind by the flow of my tears and toil ...

The rivers that run through the valleys of my heart continue to nurture a tough civilisation held together by unconditional faith ...

I represent a unique Sangam (Confluence) of wilderness, domesticity, and spirituality, and despite my heart of stone and wild soul, I always find a way to love myself more than you ever can.

And I can see how difficult it would be for someone like you to love someone like me."

– Neetisha Verma

Armed with such lofty and uplifting intentions and hoping to chance upon at least some fraction of it, I took a flight to return to Ladakh once again. As usual, I found myself flying over brown mountains that gradually turned white with a snow cover replacing the brownness of their beauty as the time ticked with certain continuity. But it also felt sometimes during the flight that time had come to a standstill as if in a balancing act of the aircraft moving forward and mountains going backwards. And surprisingly this time, I felt a familiar uneasiness in the flight itself. It was real and it was confirmed when the pilot drew our attention to it. Beyond a time, it was a flight of endless maneuvering to finally find an entry valley to Leh.

Leh's airport stood like a solitary sentinel against the backdrop of towering mountains. The moment I set foot on the tarmac, the cool breeze whispered stories of Ladakh's ancient past and spiritual mystique. As I breathed in the thin air, I could feel the altitude gently reminding me of its presence. The crisp environment was laden with a sense of anticipation. It was the beginning of an extraordinary travelling in Ladakh - The journey that would not only introduce me to the majestic landscapes of Ladakh but also lead me on an inner exploration, a journey of acclimatisation to both the altitude and unique rhythm of life in this high-altitude region.

I was well prepared for the effects of high altitude – the potential headaches, dizziness, and the importance of taking things slow. My first two days in Ladakh were dedicated to acclimatisation, and that meant letting go of my usual pace and expectations. I took a leisurely stroll around Leh, allowing the sights, sounds, and sensations of this new environment to seep into my consciousness.

As I navigated the first two days in Ladakh, acclimatisation became a metaphor for more than just adjusting to the altitude.

It was about adapting to a new pace, a new way of interacting with the world around me. The altitude reminded me to slow down, to listen to my body, and to be present in each moment. The sights and sounds of Ladakh were like whispering of wisdom, urging me to embrace this different rhythm of life. In a world where speed and efficiency often dominate, Ladakh's unhurried pace was a refreshing change. It taught me the art of slowness – of taking time to savour a cup of butter tea, of gazing at the mountains without an agenda, of engaging in conversation that meandered like Indus, Shyok, and Zanskar. Acclimatisation was, in essence, a lesson in mindfulness.

Beyond the physical adjustments, acclimatisation was also about attuning my mind and heart to Ladakh's beauty and stories. It was about cultivating an openness to the unfamiliar, letting go of preconceived notions, and allowing Ladakh to reveal itself in its own time and way. Each step and each breath were an opportunity to acclimatise not only to the thin air but also to the richness of Ladakh's landscapes, cultures, and tales.

The last time when I came to Ladakh, it was more about fun and viewing. But this time around I had decided to observe as a Novaturient Solivagant and experience the wonders of this land of Lamas and internalise the external in whatever way possible. Ladakh is one of the best places to wander in the world in the strictest sense of total Awargi.

This time I wanted to go beyond the one-dimensional cliched portrayal of this land and I set my mind to travel freely over Ladakh, the whole of Ladakh once again. My mind was receptive to capturing the magic of this isolated land and the uniqueness of a threatened way of life as if to draw me far into its diverse wonders and cull out an emotional surge to be in this one of the most beautiful places on our planet Earth.

Ladakh which means the land of high passes is situated amidst a series of High Himalayan Ranges. On the North, it is bounded by the lofty Karakoram Ranges which separate Ladakh from the Chinese District of Kotan. On its East and South East are the Chinese Districts of Rudok and Chumurti; while on its South lie the great Himalayan Ranges that separates it from Lahaul and Spiti Valleys of Himachal Pradesh.

The Southern Mountain Ranges prevent rain-bearing monsoon clouds from crossing into Ladakh, making it a rain shadow zone. The luxuriant greenery of Kullu Valley ends abruptly after crossing Rohtang Pass, and similarly, the lush green valley of Kashmir fades into barren landscapes after crossing Zoji La.

Ladakh is characterized by lofty mountain ranges and valleys with elevation varying between 9000 and 25000 feet above mean sea level. The scarcity of rain and extreme altitudes make it a difficult territory for human existence. Its snow-covered ranges, rocky edges, the astonishing colours of granite edifices rising up to the blue sky, barren terrain, sandy plains, and harsh ultraviolet radiations coupled with lack of vegetation give it a unique, out-of-the-world look.

I was determined to view beyond those beautiful looks and to begin the journey into my heart, I set course from Leh – Khardung La – Diskit – Hunder – Partapur – Tang Tse – Pangong Tso – Rezang La – Hanle – Hemis – Leh. This was the journey into my heart and to put it in the words of Mark Twain once again, it had to be fatal to my prejudice, bigotry, and narrow-mindedness. It was, therefore, imperative that I had a broad, wholesome, and charitable view of men and things. That was kind of entering a time warp as I set forth for a sojourn through Leh and Nubra Valleys.

The sun climbed up the Eastern sky to bring warmth to the chilly dawn in Leh. This time around massive road construction activities were taking place in the whole of

Ladakh and to that extent, most of the journey had to be cross country. Our Innova trudged uphill along boulder-dotted roads of dusty Himalayas. Almost two hours of teeth-chattering ride later, I reached the highest point of the trip – Khardung La at 17982 feet. Khardung La greeted me with a cold embrace, as the snowflakes of snow rain showered down on me.

As I crossed Khardung La and eased into Nubra Valley, it was a journey in transition. In the cold climes of Ladakh, flora needed human tendering to flourish. When the riverbanks showed signs of vegetation, I knew inhabitation was nearby. Standing at 10,350 feet, Diskit is the most important town in Nubra Valley. Tucked away in obscurity and fenced by the Himalayas, Nubra Valley proffered a landscape of extremes. The valley sprang to life on the fertile banks of Shyok River, a tributary of Indus River. The gilded 32-metre statue of Maitreya Buddha emerged as an unmissable landmark in Nubra Valley.

As I continued my journey onwards to Hunder, the green of Diskit was gradually being replaced with scintillating silver. Parallel to the road, running like a river of white sand, the coldest desert gave me company. Moving further, I entered the sand dunes area. The sun's rays were still oblique in the Western Sky. Waves of sand had swollen up throughout the desert in a perfectly synchronised interlude.

The high mountains were bedecked with a crown of white snow, overlooking the barren land, losing them bit by bit to contribute more mass to the desert. Thorny shrubs jut their prickly heads in some stretches. The ribbon-thin Shyok River outlining the desert often received some thirsty visitors, the double-humped Bactrian Camels. As we speeded up for Partapur, the evening too was progressing fast. The Eastern Mountains were illuminated, but the rest of the desert went under the cathedral shadow of the Western Hills. The light and shadow cut through the silhouette of the passing Army Convoy. The unfolding scene made me wonder as if I was teleported to yet another paradigm.

Climb the Mountain Within

"The place to improve the world is first in one's own heart and head, and hands, and then work outward from there. I do not climb the mountains for Nirvana. I climb them because mountains push me beyond my self-imposed limits and allow me to grow both mentally and physically. There I feel accomplished and inspired. The journey reminds me of the power of perseverance and the profound connection I can forge with Nature and those around me. No one is special there. I climb mountains to make my legs ache with pride; and return more disciplined, sharper, and grounded."

The next day I drove for Pangong Tso through the Shyok Valley. The valley surprisingly got wider and that took away any kind of claustrophobia I might have endured in the high mountains. The road meandered running at places right on the bed of Shyok. I was lucky to spot some rare wildlife. At first, I spotted a couple of stripped partridges, google called them Chukar Partridges. Then I saw a marmot, a burrowing animal of the rodent family. A very cute, dumb animal that makes it easy to prey upon, now features in the list of endangered species. The snow leopards thrive on these; marmots go; the leopards go; goes a saying. And this time, to my good luck, I even spotted many herds of white assess. They look so pristine; these are the purest forms of wildlife there. A local notion prevails in Ladakh, if humans touch those equines, their purity will be violated and they will be infected.

But for me, the standout experience through the journey was that I was finding peace within even while being thrown and tossed around during more than 500 km of jerky off-tracking for most of the journey through Ladakh. The off-tracking was not the choice but the compulsion of infra upgrade in Ladakh. And then there were strong spirals of sand in a series of whirlwinds. That was the most unlikely scenario of experiencing tranquillity. But it happened and that's the magic of mountains.

Somewhere in that interesting journey, we reached Pangong Tso. The experience there was no less than divine, nothing short of it, and a very strong gush of very cold winds welcomed me. The strong winds slapped me on my face with some force, my eyes watered, my nose froze in cold, and my senses became receptive to experiencing the vim and kindling of life. That was a kind of whack on the side of my head to goad me into accepting life as it came and keep moving on. The force of those icy cold winds was so strong that I felt my pain being pushed out of my being. Pangong Tso Lake was breathtakingly beautiful. The turquoise expanse of water, guarded by golden-lit mountains with rocky faces, and a leafless barren landscape rising into spotlessly deep blue sky enticed me to drown my sufferings in the lake and regain my sweet spot of serenity and get a glimpse of my virgin nature. I camped by the side of the lake for the night. That was really very tough, but it freed me from my mental agony and inspired me to embrace my life once again.

Pangong Tso is one of the largest, highest, and one of most beautiful lakes in the world with an average depth of one hundred metres. It's deep and steep. But alas, the glacial lake is hung, it's morbid … Is that really beautiful? I think it is. More than being beautiful, it is compassionate. It had, perhaps, accepted so much of human pain and tears that its pure glaciated waters have become brackish like that of oceans. Both Pangong Tso and the oceans absorb tons of human pain poured into them by a sea of sad humanity over the ages. Oceans still support life, but Pangong Tso doesn't. Because Pangong Tso is more compassionate!! It absorbs more human tears!

Having spent the night on the banks of Pangong Tso, I set course to Hanle.

On my way to Hanle, I stopped at Rezang La which is a mute testimony to a saga of grit, guts, and glory of the Indian Army where one of the bloodiest and most brutal conventional battles was fought during 1962, and 114 Indian Soldiers made the supreme sacrifice at the altar of our great nation. They fought valiantly and killed more than a thousand Chinese soldiers before they slept in eternal peace.

While paying a grateful tribute to soldiers at the Rezang La War Memorial, I offered more tears in tribute than those I drowned in Pangong Tso. And the spirits of The Indian Soldiers returned my tears as a sense of pride and reminded me of my duty as a soldier to myself. The pain that I carried to Ladakh vanished in the strengths of soldiering.

One of the most poignant quotes I read at Rezang La was, "They who sleep beneath the grass of green and whose earthly bodies can no longer be seen, cannot hear the ceremonies held in honour of their giving, it seems that remembrance is a salve only for the living. A last earthly measure that can be to comrades given and keeps on honouring those with soldiers sleeping." That made so much more sense to those who have suffered the loss of their loved ones.

It felt so much better seeing the radiant faces of Brave Indian Soldiers who stand solid at one of the most difficult and inhospitable frontiers of our country. The smile on their suntanned faces is the best in this universe. Soldiering moves on with elan and pride. And so must I.

After paying a tearful tribute to fallen soldiers at Rezang La, I moved on towards Hanle. Hanle was an unforgettable gateway to ecstasy where the highest density of the brightest stars illuminated my senses and rejuvenated my spirits … That view will remain etched in my mind to light up my heart forever.

Having spent two days at Hanle, I set course to Hemis and by afternoon that day, reached Hemis Monastery. The Monastery is tucked higher up into a cleavage of cliffs. It overlooked a hermitage with a cluster of smaller houses for devotees and seekers to live and delve. The atmosphere at Hemis Monastery that day was electrifying. The monks in red dresses were preparing for a function that was scheduled a week later. The rhythmic movements of Monks in cham dance accompanied by music played by them using traditional Tibetan musical instruments was a spectacle of spiritual energies that enriched the entire environment and filled every heart with joy.

Though I was not untouched by spirituality, the moment I stepped inside the Stupa (Buddhist Shrine), where a huge, towering, copper-gilded Buddha sat in a lotus mode, I had an incredible experience once again. The air was filled with smoky incense, that purified my inner realm and it felt like I was diving into the depths of a deep ocean of peace. I sat down involuntarily in the shadow of Buddha, slowly submerged myself in the chanting of hymns, and felt divinity touch me. I couldn't offer anything that was not given to me by God, but I still decided to offer my pain and suffering because there was an oblique chance that I earned them through my Karma. And I actually found my pain and sufferings leaving me and I found myself becoming feather-light, floating in the sea of serenity.

I was tired after some seven-hour drive from Hanle, and I slipped into a deep meditative slumber almost instantaneously. I effortlessly went into a trance or perhaps a waking dream and experienced a sense of calm surely descend into me. That was a kind of spiritual knock on my subconscious mind to assure me of a way forward that would permanently get me out of my gloom. The memories of seeing Vrishti's dead face were gradually getting replaced with the pleasing memories of a playful and beautiful Vrishti laughing and bubbling with energy. That was the point from where my loneliness was upgraded to aloneness and solitude became accessible.

My journey culminated in reaching a breathtaking summit, where the panorama before me seemed to mirror the height, I had scaled within myself. Ananda, a monk I was acquainted in Gompa, had spoken some very powerful words during our brief conversation on spirituality. His words echoed in my mind, "The peaks you conquer within are far more significant than any mountains you climb." As I stood at that vantage point, I realised that the journey through Ladakh had been a reflection of my spiritual ascent. The trek through Ladakh had evolved beyond a physical dimension; it had become a pilgrimage of the soul. The mountains had whispered their ancient wisdom and the monk had illuminated paths of insights to be discovered within myself.

I felt as if I was being renewed. Teleporting to that unknown level as such was a change of spiritual stratagem from where I was experiencing at a different horizon. I felt, midstream through the journey, that I was beginning to see something other than what my eyes were actually seeing. I realised the essence of nature is to move from outer to inner, and the process of internalising the impressions of the outer upon my heart and mind offered me a shift of my vantage point. The heart-mind connect, is best described in Lafcadio Hearn's lovely phrase, "The heart of things" silently speaking deep into my soul. And I was listening, loud and clear!! To view nature from that vantage point was like witnessing a meaning in making, a meaning that lies in the transformation of material into sublime.

That transformation was not a result of viewing, but the result of nature offering itself to my view, a view of will and forces of an intangibly imagined or real universe. That probably happened because the nature of nature is unself-consciousness.

And that's the magnificence, majesty, and mystery of the mighty mountains – Intimidating, inspiring, and yet so unpredictable that only the dearest of friends and the fiercest of foes would dare to visit.

I have been to many oceans and there might be so many of them in the past that many of our ancestors would have visited. Many of them are now extinct because, during the process of evolution, they have turned upside down in many places of the world to form vast deserts and mighty mountains. Ladakh is one such place where you see an ocean has done bottom up. That's the scale at which nature changes, outgrows, and renews itself for good. We, humans, have no status or right to make the mess of the minutest changes we encounter in our lives. Is it fair? Is it intelligent? Is it even logical?

Solitude Serendipity

"Solitude isn't loneliness, Solitude is when the entire serene universe seems to surround you and hold you quietly ..."

– Victoria Erickson

Ladakh for me was a complete transformation. The insights and experiences I earned there are mine forever. But they don't come with any warranty or guarantee. That means I am still entitled to her memories and I can feel them trickle down my cheeks.

Vrishti came into my life just to teach me how to live alone. Ladakh was the ocean, maybe turned upside down, and there I took a deep dive into the delight of being alone. When I was thrown back on the surface I was granted the boon of Solitude. Solitude is the summing total of my wandering, my Awargi, during my entire life.

I travelled in Arunachal Pradesh and Nagaland in a state of unawareness. When I touched awareness in Ladakh, I became aware of my experiences in oceans, mountains, plains, air, and deserts as a throwback memory. And all insights of my life were condensed in the blessing of solitude. Like a fridge magnet, I wear solitude in my heart.

On the evening before I had to take a flight back home, I sat down to have coffee all by myself and I walked in to sit with me, and that was the best company I ever had for coffee. I have enough memories of drinking coffee all by myself in a café so empty yet so crowded with the ghosts of those who have left but always stayed. But that evening all the ghosts disappeared and there was no one between us, me and myself, in that crowded Café Coffee Day in the market of Leh.

I earned solitude from Ladakh and I am eternally blessed.

People these days are nervous about being in solitude. They want noise, chatter, and unnecessary conversation, which are so often banal, inane, and vapid. That's why you often see people in airports and railway stations pulling out their mobiles and making meaningless conversations instead of reading a book or being in silence.

In the inane act of living, a man afraid of mortality seeks company, insane conversations, and groupings. Man fears lest he should face the unavoidable truth that he came into this world alone. This is his singular journey. It's on him to make or mar it. Often, we need silence and solitude to sort out our inner moorings and steer the ship of life along its true journey. It is a journey of courage and conviction, far from the machinations of the maddening crowd, to listen to that inner voice that we have quelled in pursuit of pleasure and assumed imagination of self-importance.

Everyone needs solitude to comprehend that she or he is the captain of the ship of life and the master of her or his destiny. Persian mystic Hakim Sanai says that every individual's inner self is naturally drawn to solitude. Still, living in this boisterous world, we get accustomed to chaos and start liking noise as an ineluctable option. Our inner voice doesn't gel with the noise of the world.

Our true self and inner rhythm militate against all that's shambolic and vociferous. Nobody but the individual is responsible for the onward journey. For this individualistic sojourn, we need serene solitude. The sound travels afar in solitude, one cannot even listen to one's own voice in the noise.

There is no need for fear or favour in a soulful, sole journey in solitude. It calls for solitary onward rowing. Sooner we take the first step, the better. The cosmic dance begins today, nay at this very moment. Solitude is subtle and divinity resides in subtleties. I feel solitude is beatitude where a state of perfect serenity of divinity resides. At the same time, a state of perfect solitude evokes a deep sense of gratitude.

Sometimes, there are moments in life when you just don't want to engage with anyone, not because you're ignoring them, but because you crave solitude and desire nothing but peace to recharge and reconnect with your inner self. And there is something in these moments that is simply priceless. It was the call of my solitude that night when I left Narkanda even in unkind weather because I was destined to meet you. Purpose or no purpose, it was a blessing of my solitude.

In a world that never stops buzzing, where smartphones sing their constant siren songs and FOMO lurks around every corner, there exists an art – a quiet, exquisite art – often overlooked. It's the art of solitude, the marvelous ability to find contentment in one's own company. In a society that often equates solitude with loneliness, I decided to embark on a whimsical journey to rediscover the joy of being alone.

Imagine, if you will, a grand concert hall where the world's greatest orchestra plays a symphony, yet only a few are present to hear it. Solitude, much like this scenario, is an unseen masterpiece. It's in the hush of a library, the rustling of leaves, the tick of a clock. Solitude is the symphony of self, where you are both the composer and the audience.

Picture this: a candlelit dinner, soft music in the background, and you, gazing deeply into your own eyes. Self-date nights are the quirkiest and most endearing way to experience the art of solitude. You become your own music, your own chef, and your own charmer. Who says you need a partner for a night of romance?

In a world of solitude, conversations take on a whole new dimension. You're no longer bound by societal norms or polite small talk. Instead, you can chat with the stars, engage in a profound tete-a-tete with your inner thoughts, and even strike up debates with your bookshelf. Solitude, you see, is the birthplace of unfiltered, honest dialogue.

Ever wonder why artists, writers, and inventors have a penchant for solitude? It's because, within its cocoon, creativity flourishes. Solitude offers the blank canvas upon which your wildest ideas can be painted. No distractions, no judgements – just the unfettered imagination, ready to soar to new heights.

Nature, in all its grandeur, becomes your private theatre in the world of solitude. The rustling of leaves, the symphony of the birds, and the whispering breeze become your companions. There's an intimacy in these moments with nature that can only be fully embraced when you're alone, an experience that feeds the soul.

Solitude isn't just about being alone; it's about finding yourself in that solitude. It's the time to reflect, to ponder life's mysteries, and to uncover the depths of your character. It's a journey of self-discovery where you emerge not as a solo wanderer but as a seasoned explorer of your own soul.

Solitude is the way to proceed to the quest that takes you to yourself. In solitude, you realise you only belong to yourself.

So, my dear Shibra, in the realm of solitude, embrace this quest with open arms. It's a gentle reminder that being alone is not a curse but a canvas, a stage, and an orchestra all in one. Solitude is where you dance to your own rhythm, laugh at your own jokes, and savour life on your own terms. It's the quiet rebellion against the noise of the world, a celebration of self, and a rediscovery of the joy of being alone.

Shibra liked the devotion with which Nuvem narrated his sojourn through Ladakh and his introduction to the subtle art of solitude. She also figured out the path Nuvem had taken to be him and be what he was before Vrishti went. But was that even possible? Moreover, she felt the entire experience of Nuvem was both impractical and theoretical. Multi-faceted life is too big for one solution to fit all its challenges. And deep thoughts are nothing but an escape mechanism. You can't hide behind insights and solitude instead of facing up to the tests of life.

Shibra couldn't hold her anxiety and curiosity any longer and she asked, "You mean you have found a solution to all your problems, emotional upheavals, and tormenting memories in solitude?"

Nuvem was expecting that response because during his narration of the merits of wandering he had observed Shibra looking quite lost and even out of sync. He replied, "No, no, No one is entitled to that luxury. I have worked very hard to earn my solitude, it's only a feeling, a personal experience, and a method for me to contemplate and then follow my heart without worrying about an outcome. I am in a contended phase of my life and I have reached a stage where I find peace in doing nothing! Mind you, I really slogged for it in my time.

Having said that, you can follow your heart and proceed anyway with or without spiritual or psychological aid. Following your heart is important because outcomes are always chosen for you. Always remember, as I have said before, you are only a doer and not the reason but you aren't in this universe without reason.

You have an advantage of age over me and that's a blessing. I will tell you how – You are young, you are a powerhouse of youthful energies, you are productive, you have responsibilities to fulfill, and you have to restart and take charge of your life. Your path is well defined and course charted where you don't need the crutches of solitude, wandering, or for that matter, any abstractions of deep thoughts that thwart your endeavour to do your duty, and take care of your mother, your business, and yourself.

Don't be afraid of jumping because you will surely grow wings en route. Just go and make a difference.

Glimmers

"Let those sparkles of hope keep shining even when life seems dark."

The next morning Shibra woke up fully rested and duly charged. She was peaceful and that happened to her after a long time and she was cheerful. That charming feeling was precious and she felt protected. Shibra looked around for Depression and Loneliness, but they were nowhere to be found. There was something in Fagu. What was that? Where was the trigger? No, perhaps, it was the opposite of that. She had to cherish that feeling to step out of the cocoon of her suffering.

What was happening to her? Positivity was seeping into her from everywhere. She was seeing Glimmers - the small moments that spark joy or peace, which can make her nervous system feel safe and calm. Those micro-moments discovered themselves for Shibra and made her feel joy, happiness, peace, and gratitude.

Suddenly, sunsets began to take her breath away, she savoured the taste of her apples, started to feel the breeze against her skin, and many such feel-good moments to delight herself in her own smile and she stopped brooding. Unlike that Delhi elevator experience, this time when she looked into the mirror, she saw herself, the original Shibra, she recognised her, she was beautiful, and not afraid of seeing herself in the mirror anymore. She thought for a moment what if she could train her brain to be on the lookout for glimmers, maybe more of these tiny moments will begin to appear and make her happy.

Will she have to meditate for that, seek spirituality? No, she has to do her duty sincerely because action is the source of glimmers in life. It was that simple!

Shibra suddenly remembered a story that her father had told her once. It was attributed to Rumi perhaps to give credence. The story went like this, "There was a man who sought the wisdom of a great sage, hoping to find a way to escape his suffering. The sage looked at the man and said, 'I will help you, but first, you must do something for me. Take this spoon, fill it with oil, and walk through the town, without spilling a drop.'

The man thought this task was simple enough and agreed. He took the spoon, filled it with oil, and walked through the town. As he carefully balanced the spoon, he couldn't help but focus all his attention on not spilling any oil.

When he returned to the sage, the sage asked, 'Did you see the beautiful flowers in the town square? Did you notice the children playing and the laughter of the families?' The man realised he had been so fixated on the spoon that he hadn't noticed anything else.

The sage then said, 'This is the key to dealing with pain. Just as you were so focused on the spoon that you missed the beauty around you, when you are consumed by the suffering, you miss the beauty of life. Pain is like the spoon, and life is like the town. Don't let the pain consume your entire focus.

Remember to look around and appreciate the beauty that still exists.'

The man understood the sage's message – while pain and suffering are part of life, it's essential not to let them overshadow the beauty and joy that can be found in a moment."

The story serves as a reminder that even in the pain, there is an opportunity to find meaning and beauty in moments.

Shibra knew she was beautiful, intelligent, talented, and sensitive. But she was different. Different in a way that she always wanted more from life. She was headstrong and intractable and her parents knew never to oppose but to guide her into doing something that they thought was good for her. So, such stories were a part of her life and she exactly knew what they were meant for. They sometimes worked well for her. The fact that she remembered her father while trying to uplift herself became a glimmer.

Her father over-loved her to the extent that her elder sister often accused her dad of partiality. Noor, her elder sister, felt deprived, cheated, and hurt by her dad's behaviour. Noor was a super sensitive child and she didn't understand why Dad had to favour Shibra every time. But Zainab, her mother was overly protective of her and she was a psychological support for Noor. Shibra often boasted of her chemistry with her father, but Zainab ensured that Noor was never deprived of her dad's love.

Today, Noor is happily settled in the US, she loves her father. Shibra misses him and she is struggling to find her feet once again in life. And Zainab??? Isn't she lonely? And left alone to fend for herself. She was the best thing that happened to their family. She was their Glimmer. Does she deserve to be sad about Shibra?

Shibra suddenly thought of Nuvem. Is he a Glimmer? Is Salim Khan messaging her through Nuvem Verma? There could be no such connection, but when Shibra decides to think that way who can stop her? And for that matter, anyone can decide to think whatever! And what if, her meeting with Nuvem was a part of destiny?

Shibra smiled and somehow wriggled out from the cosy snuggle of her comforter and came out. Nuvem was sitting quietly in front of the fireplace with a cup of tea. Some familiar and beautiful Bengali "Bishti-Mishti" song was playing softly.

Shibra couldn't help humming a similar old Hindi song of which she remembered the tune but not the words. Nuvem smiled and said, "Tum Pukar Lo …" from a movie I still love, "Khamoshi starring Waheeda Rehman and Rajesh Khanna."

He remembered fondly, "This is from a Bengali Movie 'Deep Jwele Jaai – 1959. Khamoshi came in 1970 and Hemant Kumar composed music for both the movies. It brings tears to my eyes whenever I listen to this, don't know why, especially when I see Suchitra Sen who plays the role of a mentally disturbed patient in the movie. The character 'Nurse Mitra' was a short story written by Ashutosh Mukherji on which both films were based and both the films were directed by Asit Sen. Khamoshi was a little bit more melodramatic whereas 'Deep Jwele Jaai' was more realistic."

Shibra stopped smiling and that didn't go unnoticed by Nuvem. He felt guilty of inadvertently touching the wrong chords. He immediately made amends, said nothing but just held her hand for a few moments, and asked, "Some ginger tea for you?"

There was for sure an assuredness in that touch and Shibra got her smile back. That morning was beautiful because there was no storm in her mind. She loved the feeling. She was looking at Nuvem with gratitude and her feelings reached him. He felt he was with his daughter. And he too loved the feeling.

Hiraeth – A Nostalgic Longing

"Hiraeth beckons with wordless call, hear, my soul with heart enthralled;

Hiraeth whispers while earth I roam; Here I wait for the call 'come home' ..."

– Tim Davis

Shibra looked out of the window. It was a clear day, the sun was behind her and while the cottage was in the shade, the landscape before her was lit by the sun's rays. The view of the valley enchanted her. She simply stood quietly admiring the wonders of nature and slowly slipping into contemplation of the majesty of creation.

Nuvem observed her for a moment, then let her be and continued reading a book on Mount Kailash by Davinder Bhasin, the younger brother of his friend Balraj Bhasin. There wasn't any oddity in the silence of the room because both Shibra and Nuvem were in their respective zones, unmindful of everything. The silence was breached when Keenie called them for breakfast.

After breakfast, while Shibra wanted to go on a trek, Nuvem was happy to relax and read. Shibra changed and came out into the chill of the air and serenity of the nature. She had nothing particular in her mind, all options were open, but surprisingly she preferred to walk up to Deshu Mata temple on Fagu Top. She went to the temple and thereafter sat in the same spot where she sat with Nuvem the other day.

Nuvem felt a bit apprehensive about letting her go alone and all by herself. Shibra appeared to be gaining her confidence, but given the fragile state of her mind, he wasn't sure about her. She just met him a few days ago, yet he found a certain bond building between them. The bond that began in pain was gradually growing into one of mutual affection. Unknowingly Nuvem was being overprotective of Shibra. A strange but beautiful relationship was firming between both of them.

Nuvem had organised a driver to escort her home to Dehradun. But on hearing about going back, she panicked and pleaded for some more time to be with him at Fagu. Her response surprised him and he almost felt guilty for asking her to leave too soon.

Shibra sat alone on Fagu top and she missed Nuvem. She sat quietly for a few minutes and began to experience peace flowing within. While climbing up to the temple she had sweated a bit and the chilling strong winds on top made her feel very cold. And yet she wanted to sit there alone. She pulled out and wore her jacket and that made her feel comfortable.

As her mind became calm, Zainab appeared in her thoughts. Zainab had lost her companion and support, yet she tried to be a pillar of support to Shibra and cared for her needs, both spoken and unspoken. Shibra was a true copy of Zainab in every way of her life; she wore an uncanny resemblance to

Zainab in her face, her behaviour, her etiquette, her attitude, her ethics, morale, and her manners. And yet Shibra forgot to trust Zainab who loved her unconditionally, and became even more caring after the demise of Salim Khan. After her dad passed away and Shameer Sikander broke her heart into pieces, her mother forgot her sufferings and became the source of her strength. But Shibra just left her alone when Zainab needed her the most. Shibra felt ashamed of being so ungrateful, self-centred, and selfish. She wanted to reach out to her mother. Tears flooded her eyes and she cried for a long time sitting alone in that unknown but kind place.

Shibra had always taken her mother for granted and she loved to be spoiled by her dad. Dad and she were always a team and Zainab never let Noor be neglected or deprived of her father's affection. Noor was an emotional and sensitive child and depended on Zainab for everything. After Noor shifted to the US, Zainab missed her a lot and felt lonely a lot of times.

Zainab treated her daughters as equals though Noor attracted more of her support. And Zainab stood steadfast on her principles. She believed Shibra needed more tendering till she turned eighteen. But the wild ways of Shibra always kept her on her toes. Salim Khan wanted her to excel in whatever field she chose and he involved her in running their family business. Shibra excelled in academics and her business acumen was above average. She spoke well, her written and verbal expressions and consulting capabilities were excellent, and she was a genuine leader. But Zainab was worried about her because she knew Shibra was an overthinking perfectionist and an erratic genius.

Both Salim and Zainab were proud of her. Though Shibra remained in the limelight for all the good reasons, Zainab, for some unknown reasons, was very insecure about her. Zainab was aware that even the best women professionals would find it extremely difficult to breach the ego domain of men because men have scripted the world to their convenience and earning a rightful place in that world would always be a difficult and distressing call for any woman of substance. Zainab believed that the surest way to success in life lay in mediocrity because it protected one from banging the egos of others. To that extent, the exceptional competence and confidence and uber-sensitive nature of Shibra left Zainab worrying all the time about her getting hurt in this unequal and unkind world for women. Shibra fell for a narcissist who used and discarded her. And after Salim's sudden cardiac arrest, Zainab's world fell apart and she also lost Shibra to Depression and Loneliness. The business became stagnant and their home empty.

Shibra had left Zainab alone when they both needed each other in the hour of their crises. She was wandering away from home for over a year and of late she was not even picking Zainab's calls. And when she did pick up her call, she hurriedly disconnected saying she would call later which she rarely did. Shibra had failed to empathise with Zainab knowing fully well that she too was in turmoil. Shibra was crying for being so ungrateful and selfish. She tried to remember Zainab's face. When she was leaving home, Shibra remembered seeing gloom and sadness written all over her mother's beautiful face. Zainab's eyes went dry, her smile vanished, and she stopped taking care of herself immediately after Salim went to his heavenly abode. Shibra didn't even tell Zainab where she was heading. That day Shibra further broke two broken hearts, her mother's and her own. Her mind had surely turned against her and her pain had silenced her sensitivity.

Shibra wondered why she became so insensitive to treat the pain and sufferings of Zainab, who had lost her companion, her lover, her friend, their business, and even her daughter, with utter disdain. How could Shibra fall prey so easily to negative emotions and close all entries of sunshine of love and positivity in her life? When she finally decided to end her life on that road bend, Nuvem came from nowhere and distracted her, but it was Zainab who appeared in her last thoughts to save her life.

The last few days of her life at Fagu were special because she had decided to dump her depression and loneliness, and that cleared the dense fog that hid her way to her home. What a beautiful thought that was, going home. The ache for home lives in all of us. The safe place where she could go as she was and not be questioned. Shibra learned in that moment that home is not a place alone, but a whole gamut of feelings. The place where they lived, her dad, mom, Noor, and she.

Was that Hiraeth - a deep and irrational bond felt with a time, era, place, or person; the feeling of longing for a home that no longer exists or never was? No, perhaps, it was a nostalgic longing to be near again to something or someone distant, or that has been loved and then lost; "the love that remains."

Shibra didn't want to intellectualise or complicate it by overthinking. She had to be intellectually humble and experience the curious joy of being wrong, be open to new information, and be willing to change her attitude and mind to a newer simplicity.

Moment Shibra opened her mind, she heard the calm and soothing voice from within, "You choose for yourself and I will choose for you. But what I choose for you will be final. If you surrender to my wish, I shall grant even that what you want. But if you resist what I choose for you, I will ensure you never get what you want, and eventually what I chose for you will happen for you. Now go return to your mother and clear the mess you have created."

She surrendered and requested, "pave a path that must exist." Just then her mom spoke in her, "Old faces come knocking at my door. Searching for the girl who lived here before. I tell them she's been gone for a while. She's been sent off into exile. Her crime was she gave a little too much. She bled until she was empty. Giving to those who wished her misery. Foolish of her to think it was love. Don't bother waiting for her to return. She is no longer your concern. She doesn't live here anymore."

Shibra was continuously crying and just then she felt a palm over her eyes from behind that was not just warm. It had the softness of a prayer, a familiar touch, something she had almost forgotten. The palm felt like mom's. In that quiet moment, she realised; she truly loved her mom.

And Shibra drifted into the pleasures of peace and serenity of her mind after a long, long time.

TAKING STRANGER HOME

"Everything happens for a reason. Everything. Your highs. Your lows. Your happiest moments and the most painful ones. Your failures and your successes. Your losses and your gains. Just remember – people can't walk in and out of your life for no reason. The lesson you learn and the growth that you experience is never spontaneous. It's always meant to be. There's a higher purpose. A goal. A final destination, or a peak in your journey that you will have no idea of until you reach it. But for that – you need to climb the mountain. For that – you need to look for a deeper meaning. For that – you need to pay attention to everything and everyone around you, especially those that love you and leave you. There are some lessons that only people and their existence can give you. There are some lessons that only pain can bring out. There are some lessons that the biggest joys of your life will reveal to you. And there are some lessons that you never knew were lessons until they walked out of your life. Think about it – only then will you stop treating your growth as an accident and start appreciating it as the most beautiful journey created just for you."

– @r.dhalwriter

Shibra wanted to stay a little longer at Fagu. She was falling in love with both Fagu and Nuvem. She met Nuvem during her bout of most dangerous vulnerability and he brought her to Fagu. That was serendipity because she discovered something in Fagu and Nuvem's company that reaffirmed her desire to detach from loneliness and depression. She was still apprehensive about her ability to sustain her resolve, but she loved the feeling sans those goons in her life. She felt much relieved and genuinely happy. She had broken the trap of unnecessary illusion around her. However, that fragility was no justification for not wanting to leave Fagu. It was already seven days since she came there and though he did not make her feel that way even Nuvem knew that they had overstayed the hospitality of Bhasins because of her.

Both of them were comfortable in their company. Shibra didn't want to leave him. She even natured the thought of taking him home. She wanted him to escort her to Dehradun. She felt safe in his company. What she liked about him was he was not a preachy old man and he wasn't awkward with her and she loved that familiarity. He was as loving and generous with her as her father, Salim Khan and she loved this man becoming the centre of her attention for the moment. As that affection sank into her psyche, her daughterly or more importantly, her womanly instinct to exercise exclusivity over her man came to the fore and she didn't like his over-involvement with his mobile phone and whiskey.

That evening when they met, she finally asked, "Isn't your involvement with your phone and liquor toxic?"

Nuvem replied, "Toxicity of living is injurious to life, it's not whiskey, my dear."

"Isn't it weird that you are continually fiddling with your mobile and sipping whiskey? And what about me who is sitting with you and vying for both your attention and affection?"

Nuvem was as surprised by her question as he was convinced of the authenticity of her thought. He perhaps underestimated Shibra's genuine affection for him because she was still a stranger, they just met only seven days ago, and soon they would go their ways. In any case, he had seen so many changes in his life that he had learnt to be comfortable with changes, and more importantly, with the power of the change in decimating the notion of permanence on a daily basis. Simultaneously a stray thought crossed his mind of familiarity of the patterns of a woman's heart which makes her susceptible to hurting herself and rendering her vulnerable to a man who has been conditioned not to equally reciprocate and understand her affection. For that reason, he will invariably take her for granted, devalue her affection, knowingly or unknowingly, and eventually alienate her from him and herself. That stray thought made him understand his guilt and grief. Guilt is the positivity of grief for it makes one realise that after all grief is nothing but unexpressed love. Or is it a manifestation of the inability of a man to value the innate love that God conveys through a woman till he is reminded by his guilt much later after he loses the best he was bestowed with and he begins to lose his will to live? That marks the beginning of the exploration of the self.

Nuvem was unusually quiet for a long time and Shibra thought she could have inadvertently hurt him or triggered a memory. She didn't want to make much out of it and sheepishly asked, "Are you okay, sir?"

Nuvem realised he had perhaps wandered too far into his thoughts and hurriedly but consciously replied, "I celebrate sitting with myself, the ambience of the environment, and an energetic company like yours which life is benevolent and magnanimous enough to grant me occasionally."

Shibra felt flattered but more impressed by his wit, and she asked him, "You don't like music?"

"I definitely love music when I am driving alone or when I am happy or I am with me but not when I am lonely. Because then, my choice of music smacks of melancholy, pain, suffering, loneliness, and longing. And in the same breath let me explain my involvement with my mobile phone which you have been asking for all the time and I have been conveniently accusing you and your generation of over-dependence on your devices.

Most of us senior citizens have become slaves of our digital devices and everyone has his or her reason for that despite such dependence being dangerous. I feel humans are no longer any intelligent, we are stupid. It is a sort of retardation that we take pride in degrading the environment, and ecology, and creating an artificial intelligence in the name of progress and prosperity. This is moral degradation, to say the least.

My mobile phone consumes me for more than five hours a day on average. Initially, my mobile phone made me feel good, but later on, it violated my nothingness which I feel is more valuable because it cherishes silence. Draconically, it decimated my time for her when she was around, at least she thought so, and perhaps, she was right. How can you love someone if they don't feel that pious emotion coming from you reach them? Now when she has departed, my mobile mocks me and dares me to leave it. My mind is also right when it asks, "Why leave it now? Doesn't it help you combat your loneliness and garner sympathy? My digital ego too chips in to adore my digital device for fooling me feel so important.

At some point in time, I surrendered my will to survive and accepted my device as my support system.

And then came a day when I realised my folly. I was lacking discipline and putting my character, identity, and privacy on display to the public view. Someone from within said sternly, that if you are looking to tackle your pain and loneliness in your mobile phone, it's like sleeping with your enemy. It also reminded me that I had forgotten living, wasted my time binge-watching a lot of unproductive stuff and I was distancing myself from my loved ones who cared for me and for whom I cared. Self-introspection triggered itself and with discipline, I reduced my screen time on my mobile phone to one hour per day on average. The only time it goes up is when I write because I save my thoughts and ideas in my notes as and when they come."

"So, you are into digital detox?"

"No, I have been trying consciously, though without much success, to break up with it and for good. I am prepared to embrace even boredom. This is helping me repair my fractured relationships with myself. I am feeling much better."

"Will your fragile resolve survive?"

"There is no compromise. It's all the compassion that needs commitment, discipline, and love for our loved ones, and more importantly for ourselves. I need to value love which still enriches me. I certainly don't want my digital devices to fracture my solitude."

Shibra was deeply into reel mania and she watched them a lot of time. She heard him patiently, not because of what he was saying, but why he was saying. She assumed that he seemed to have become addicted to his mobile phone and habitually consumed a lot of useless stuff on it. Like every man of his generation, he too was in love with his mobile and she doubted if he would be able to honour his commitment for long.

She smiled and it was like, 'Nuvem you are fooling yourself' and said, "I don't understand much of your breaking up with your mobile. You can always throw it and it will break, but that won't break your relationship with it. If you mean your commitment to love, you have to break up your unhealthy habits. Every one of us is succumbing to the fetish and voyeurism of our inner addictions and is being consumed by habits and not devices. So, if you want to move to better depth and quality of life, try and conquer your habits, it will be more difficult though, at your age and stage.

I feel you can do it because you are heavily investing in alternatives. Be mindful because the line between wandering and escapism is thin, if not blurred. I will see you as my inspiration because mine rests in peace."

That last sentence that she spoke spilled out her latent pain, but she recovered immediately and said, "I am going back tomorrow, and you will leave me home."

Nuvem was happy that Hiraeth finally found Shibra, but he said "No, you will go the day after, because it's too late now and we need to organise a driver for you."

"I don't need a driver; I can drive myself. So, we leave the day after tomorrow at sharp seven and clear Shimla before eight, the rest of the drive will be fun. Goodnight."

The moment Shibra touched her back on her bed, she wanted to sleep. But someone from within asked why you want Nuvem to accompany you home. You are a solo traveller and you feel you are better off alone then why him? Why do you want to take a stranger home? How much do you know him? Why this blind trust? Do you love him?

Shibra had to cover her ears with both her palms to prevent hearing those piercing questions and so many of them troubling her. She knew she had to address those questions to be able to sleep. She decided to address the last question first and then go backwards.

"You don't need to love someone to trust him, but if you trust him, you will definitely love him. You are right I don't want Nuvem to accompany me because I am alone, but I want to take him home for my mother."

"You want a companion for your mother, did I hear you right? Hasn't he made it amply clear he is Vrishti's man?"

"Yeah, I mean, I still want him for her, not as in romantically. I know at this point in time; she needs me more. Yeah, I am guilty of not caring for her during the past three years and I want to make up for the lost time. And I want him to be there as well, maybe knowing well that he may never replace my dad in her life. But he will be a very good companion for her. So I feel, strangely though."

"You are imagining too much and you want your mother to settle down to be happy."

"Yes, my dad always believed imagination is more powerful than intelligence. And yes, let time flow and take care."

"Did you ask your mother what she wants or did you ask Nuvem? Maybe, they are happy being alone and enjoying their freedom."

"Maybe. But there is something known as destiny. I can't force them, their destiny can. And are they really free in their freedom, if both of them want that way?"

"And what about you?"

"Let time take over my fate and my life. Goodnight Shibra."

In the adjacent room, Nuvem was thinking of Shibra. Such a decent girl, he had grown fond of her in just seven days. She was well-bred, cultured, caring, and affectionate. Now that she had decided to go home, he was happy and sad. Sad because she was leaving, and happy because she was going home to her mother. Her mother would be overjoyed to see her.

Nuvem was happy to accompany her because he wouldn't have even allowed his daughter to drive alone over such a long distance from Fagu to Dehradun. And he was happier going to Dehradun and spending time in his unit which was stationed in Dehradun.

DOPPELGANGER

"I started adoring you; Ardently even more; The day I met you!! I wanted to be with you and desired to be healed by you!! With my prating talks; To regale you!! It's just because I found her Doppelganger facc in you!!"

At that time of the season, the weather was wonderful and drive pleasant. Nuvem was driving his car and Shibra from the co-driver's seat was navigating. They didn't need music because they kept conversing throughout the journey, except when Shibra fell asleep. The driver followed them in Shibra's Mercedes.

After a half-an-hour breakfast break at Dharampur and a longish lunch break at Haldirams near Muzaffarnagar, they reached Dehradun by 5:00 PM. Nuvem had planned to drop Shibra at her home and thereafter proceed to his unit. As they entered Dehradun, they waded through crawling traffic and took a turn towards the Mussoorie Road. Some ten km short of Mussoorie, they turned on a different road axis to her home on top of a hill. By the time they reached home, it was 7:00 PM and it was dark.

Nuvem wanted to drop Shibra home and drive back to Dehradun where the officers of his unit were waiting for him. Shibra would, in no way, let that happen because, after a tiring drive of approximately twelve hours, she expected him to take much-needed rest. She wanted him to meet her mother and stay the night in their home.

Zainab was in her living room and she was about to have her dinner. She was thinking of Shibra as a usual daily ritual but she wasn't expecting her as usual. Shibra hadn't even called her for a long time now. When she heard her voice that evening, she didn't believe her ears but when Shibra called again her face lit up, and she rushed down in a huff to receive her. Unmindful of Nuvem's presence, Zainab held Shibra in a bear hug. Zainab felt the warmth in Shibra's hug after a long time and they both allowed their tears to flow freely. Nuvem witnessed that beautiful moment and he silently prayed that Shibra and Zainab would heal each other.

Nuvem was a sensitive man and under normal circumstances, he would have cried seeing the intensity of affection of a mother and her child. But as he saw Zainab for the first time, he could not keep his eyes away from her beautiful face. His trance broke when Shibra introduced Zainab to him and Zainab greeted him. Zainab felt Nuvem's behaviour was abnormal but she quickly passed that as his initial hesitation of meeting someone for the first time. But she was not comfortable with the way he was almost staring at her. It was rather awkward. Nuvem too was uncomfortable till he heard Zainab giving instructions to her staff to do up his room.

Shibra led him to their sitting room for a cup of tea while the guest room was being prepared for him. She was not happy about his strange behaviour while meeting Zainab.

She didn't like the way he behaved with her mother. Why was he staring at her? But Nuvem was in his own world and he didn't notice her unhappiness. He quietly finished his tea and Shibra led him to the guest room.

By that time, Nuvem had regained some of his composure in the thought that we were not alone – at least, not our faces! He recalled having read that there are more than two of us at every stage of life. The figure may be ten or more. He truly believed God would have a reserve of one hundred archetypes each for women and men. Those archetypes should have ten variations throughout their lifetimes. Sometimes, some of us have the opportunity to confirm them at some stages of our lives. Nuvem just did it that day. He met Zainab as Vrishti's doppelganger!!

Many times, when he pointed out those discoveries of his to friends and family, they laughed it off. They don't see what he sees. Where he sees the connection, they see anonymity. Nuvem felt that eventually, over time, we all become our own doppelgangers, these completely different people who just happen to look like us!!

The memories of Vrishti flooded his mind and tears rolled down his cheeks once again. And once again, Nuvem realised that memories of her were irresistible. They were a collective expression of both heartache and hope. They were a shared experience of vulnerability and catharsis. And love. Nuvem's heart and mind were syncing up in Vrishti's memories. Sync-up is subtle and is beyond detachment. Sometimes, the emptiest places held the heaviest memories.

Shibra came to fetch him for dinner, he had not even changed and sat as she left him. He hurriedly wiped his face and tried to smile but she could sense he was sad. She had understood by then that something was not right ever since he met Zainab. But what? But before she could say anything, he showed her a photo of a pretty woman. She was wearing black trousers, a red top, a grey cardigan, black goggles, and matching sports shoes. Now it was Shibra's turn to be surprised and she couldn't believe her eyes. In the first look from a particular angle, it was puzzling to see Zainab's photo on his mobile and wallet.

A lot of unnecessary questions cropped up in her mind as she became overprotective about Zainab. How does Nuvem know her mother? Where and when did they meet? Why didn't she tell her about Nuvem? Is there a past involving them? And if so, was her father aware? Shibra's enthusiasm and exuberance of returning home disappeared almost immediately and she sat down in disbelief. The secret desire she was nursing about a possible companionship for Zainab ditched her instantaneously and it was replaced by the one of over-possessiveness about her mother. Shibra was angry at herself for trusting Nuvem. She felt cheated and disgusted.

Nuvem was observing the shades of sadness on Shibra's face and her dipping morale didn't escape his attention either. He rightly fathomed the reason for her mood swings and said, "This is Vrishti, my wife." Isn't your mother an archetype of her? Your mother's face brought back a Tsunami of memories I was hiding within and wasn't she wearing the same attire? But the moment I heard her voice, I knew she was not Vrishti, and I fought hard to gather my nerves thereafter. In a compulsion to make sure her and Vrishti's faces weren't the same, I couldn't help staring at your mother's face to the extent that she was uncomfortable. But what an uncanny resemblance! I just couldn't help, I am sorry."

Shibra sprang to her feet, she was overwhelmed by the similarity between Zainab and Vrishti and didn't know what to do, so, she hugged him tightly. That affectionate moment coincided with Zainab's entry into his room who came looking for them. Zainab knew that was Shibra's trademark gesture for expression of her happiness. But she was not sure whether Shibra should trust Nuvem so much because, after all, he was only a stranger whom she met only a few days ago. And there was always a danger of betrayal and neither Shibra nor she could afford more heartaches.

The moment she saw Zainab, Shibra released her hug on Nuvem and held Zainab lovingly behind her back as she turned to lead both of them to the dining room. The food was home cooked and that was a luxury for Nuvem. The décor of the well-laid dining room and the touch and the taste of a woman made the simple home-cooked food priceless for him. He was overwhelmed by the memories of such care way back in time when Vrishti was alive, but he managed to restrain himself remarkably well. Nuvem accepted Zainab was not Vrishti and that helped him discipline his emotions better. The gratitude of his moist eyes conveyed everything and it reached both Shibra and Zainab in equal measure. Silence always decorates unspoken words and genuine feelings.

There was an obvious air of formality and the presence of a man other than Salim Khan in her home was unnerving for Zainab. Sitting right across Zainab, even Nuvem was uncomfortable. Had there been anyone else except Zainab sitting there, Nuvem would have easily orchestrated the cordiality but he was a bit off-colour in the presence of Zainab. He was consciously trying not to look at Zainab and that was further adding to his discomfort. Zainab was obviously not aware of her resemblance with Vrishti and she was trying to be happily affectionate and a wonderful host. She was very graceful and the authenticity of the flair of Urdu language in her accent suited her delicate mannerisms. There was a perceptible warmth of loving care and the scent of a woman in her home.

In stark contrast to that homeliness, Nuvem had often heard passersby lamenting the lack of vibrancy and deficit dynamics of their home in Jaipur after Vrishti. Her unflinching and selfless commitment to her family was irreplaceable. He had decided to live with that status and made peace with it. The vibrancy of Zainab's home only highlighted the hollowness of his life after Vrishti had proceeded to her heavenly abode.

And the dynamics of Zainab's home made it crystal clear to Nuvem that women could always manage the worst situations of life remarkably better than men. He always believed that a woman is the light of her home because she so painstakingly builds her nest and puts her heart and soul into filling it with love. Nuvem tried to add vibrancy to their home by increasing the illumination of Vrishti's home, but he always wondered if the blinding lights of opulent chandeliers were actually hiding the broken fragments of his life …

And he inadvertently spoke to himself, "All men are not useless, good ones are!!!" Shibra was trying to read his feelings, and expression of helplessness, and she gauged something was amiss in the spontaneity of Nuvem's simplicity, and she knew he was drifting into an emotional trap. She became extra caring towards him and that didn't go unnoticed by Zainab. Zainab smiled in assuredness of her belief that her daughter was finally back to her life though she was yet to grasp her chemistry with Nuvem. Whatever that was, Shibra had come back happier with Nuvem and Zainab silently said her prayers of gratitude to Allah for His benevolence.

Dinner over, he thanked Zainab for putting up the sumptuous dinner at such short notice and serving the same with genuine affection. Nuvem always overdid such praises because he always underdid it when Vrishti showered so much love on him and her daughters. The mother-daughter duo escorted him to his room.

Finally, Nuvem was alone, Vrishti was all over his mind. Was his meeting with Zainab wyrd? Destined? But he was too tired to delve into those tender thoughts and he fell asleep as soon as he hit the bed.

A Cup of Tea

"When the world is all at odds; And the mind is all at sea; Then cease the useless tedium: And brew a cup of tea; There is magic in its fragrance; There is solace in its taste; And then laden moments vanish; Somehow into space; And the world becomes a lovely thing! There's beauty as you'll see; All because you briefly stopped; To brew a cup of tea."

– Anonymous

The next day he got up early, but he decided to laze around and that's where his thoughts caught up from where he had left them last night. And yes, it was Zainab who dominated them this time.

And Zainab had to be there for a striking resemblance with Vrishti. Zainab was in her early fifties, a few years younger than Vrishti, and her build, face, and sense of dressing up were very similar to Vrishti's. Only her voice wasn't as rich as Vrishti's and that was a reminder to Nuvem that Zainab was not Vrishti. He didn't have to proceed with caution because he was and will always be Vrishti's man, or so he thought.

Nuvem recollected saying to Shibra at Deshu Mata Temple in Fagu that her meeting with him was not a mere coincidence but had a purpose. Was Zainab had to do something with it? Where is life taking him? It couldn't have been only a coincidence that Zainab was wearing the same dress that Vrishti wore when they had gone to Subathu, Himachal Pradesh. Had it not been for her, Nuvem would have gone to his unit after dropping Shibra home. Why did he stay the night in her home? Was it for Zainab who he had met yesterday for the first time ever in his life? It is intriguing to realise the connection that one soul feels with another soul, kindred or otherwise. It may appear quite baffling to find a seemingly unknown or unconnected certain individual or creature appearing as known or familiar. In his case, however, the reason could be Zainab's face that was drawing him closer to her.

He didn't want to make much sense of Zainab and he got up, had a cup of tea, and came to the balcony. Theirs was a palatial bungalow sprawling over ten acres of green land. The view of the place from the balcony was mesmerising. When seen from there, the meandering meadows, bubbling creeks, the dense woods of deodar, and the distant Himalayan peaks offered a panoramic view of the landscape. When Nuvem was engrossed in witnessing a kaleidoscopic view of "The Land of God" Zainab walked into it.

She was walking with the gardener and tending to their exotic plants and beautiful flowers. Nuvem wanted to go in, but he couldn't, instead his eyes kept following her. Decency demanded he returned to his room and as he turned to go in, Zainab too turned and saw him. He wished her, she waived at him and invited him for a cup of tea with her in their manicured garden.

As he came out of his room, one helper was there to guide him to a tea table placed under a garden umbrella by the side of their glasshouse. Zainab welcomed him and they sat down to have a cup of tea with crispy coconut cookies. The beautiful morning became more beautiful in the company of a pretty woman.

He looked closely at Zainab's face as she poured tea from the pot. He felt something move in him. He was nervous and a thought crossed his mind, if she were Vrishti what would he do? "I will hug her and never let her go again," he told himself. Alas, she was not her. Zainab was as pretty as Vrishti, maybe an ounce lower. An unfair comparison because every woman is pretty and complete in her own way.

Zainab gave him the tea and said, "It's August and the air is already having a nip."

He said, "I love this beautiful weather. Our country is so diverse even in climatic conditions. Plains, back there are burning hot and it's so lovely here."

Nuvem remembered that his conversation even with Shibra began with Fagu's weather. But with Zainab, it was different because Nuvem felt an unfamiliar awkwardness of over-familiarity with her beautiful face. Doppelgangers are a statement of the omnipresence of God. He loves all humans alike and above the bounds of divisive castes, creeds, and religious beliefs. And despite the similar appearance of the Doppelgangers, each of them is unique and complete in herself or himself.

Mercifully, the weather once again became an ice-breaker and got them conversing generally beginning with her lovely and healthy plants. And then came another hiccup in his feelings when he learnt Zainab also was a Delhi University graduate from Janki Devi College which was Vrishti's alma mater as well.

As if to divert himself from overthinking the similarity between the beautiful women, he asked, "What do you do?" and he immediately regretted asking her that question because he hated people who asked him that question.

But Zainab replied without blinking, "My routine had hardly changed except that my pillar of strength has left for his heavenly abode and left me alone. I have no time, there is so much work at home."

"But you have helpers helping you do the household chores?"

Zainab smiled, "All men think alike because they don't understand that helpers only help. They do their assigned tasks faithfully, but a homemaker works beyond tasks. She sees work that no one else can. Her commitment to her home forms the emotional matrix and bonding of her family. Have you ever realised this when Vrishti Ji was around?"

That was a piercing question and it demanded courage and honesty to reply. Nuvem said, "Unfortunately, I never realised that and didn't even care much. All of us were selfish and we even didn't mind hurting her a lot of times by taking her for granted. The so-called realisation only dawned when she left and my family fragmented. We are still struggling to cope with the knowledge that things will never be the same again."

The massive surge of Vrishti's memories and his guilt almost choked him with emotions and he had to stop speaking any further to prevent them from pouring through his eyes. Nuvem had learned to control vibrations of his voice by keeping mum in such uninvited emotional surges but his eyes and facial expressions invariably betrayed him. In fact, he was always caught up in such situations without warning and the only remedy he found for that was he would stop speaking. That lack of control wasn't universal, it always manifested only with certain people for whatever reason. But why was that happening in the presence of Zainab?

And when he gathered his wits around him, he saw Zainab crying, and she did not hold back and allowed her tears to flow freely. Seeing her, one drop of a tear managed to slip out of his beleaguered eyes and bleeding heart. Suddenly, sonder, gnossienne, and saudade made sense to him in a field of the Nimbus Cloud of Unknowing. That was the SMOTH Moment.

The conversation for the morning ended abruptly, but not before connecting both of them through a bond of pain. Zainab got back to tending to her plants and he walked back to his room. Shibra was still sleeping in the comforts and security of her home, sweet home.

Is love as a bond of pain a serendipity?

The Cards We Are Dealt

"Hearts united in pain and sorrow will not be separated by joy and happiness. Bonds that are woven in sadness are stronger than the ties of joy and pleasure."

– Khalil Gibran

Once back in his room, Nuvem cried hard and drained his emotions out of his heart and mind. The words are so strange. What Zainab said, lost meaning the moment she uttered those words because Nuvem interpreted them through the filters of his perceptions. And, they hit him hard and touched his vulnerable chords of love.

Nuvem was once again teleported to a realm where he wanted to cry and only cry. Vrishti was in love with Nuvem and a woman in love gives herself beyond herself. She devotes herself to her home and family and nurtures everyone with so much giving, caring, and love that she forgets when she separates her from herself.

Somewhere in her commitment, Vrishti had lost herself in her unrequited love and Nuvem was to be blamed for that because she loved him and he never could come up to her expectations of minimal reciprocal love. Not that he didn't love her, but he hardly cared. When anyone in the family fell ill, she would go all out to support and take care, and when she was unwell, which was rare, all she would get a rude retort, "Take medicine." She hardly took medicines and even worked while in fever with no real words of concern for her. It was taken for granted that she had no right to fall sick.

She was destined to be loved by everyone except those who she loved the most. And all she wanted from him was some time for her, that's all. All that Nuvem did was hide himself in excessive work and still, she stood with him through his thick and thin. Nuvem loved her, but she didn't know! Everything is fair in the war of love though!

Both the daughters became her support system. They loved her and cared for her. But when they grew wings, Vrishti slowly drifted into loneliness. That was the time she decided to find herself, be herself, and define her happiness. But she didn't quit loving him.

And ten days before she left for her heavenly abode, she gave his report card to him, "You don't love me, you love your friends more." Those words were not true, but Nuvem truly deserved that report card of his life. She was very unwell, underconfident, complex, and frail, and the way she said those words added more truth to her conviction.

No one knew then that time was really short and Nuvem had to alter that conviction and convince her of his unadulterated love. It was already too late by then. But God loved her and wanted to take her away happier and as such gave those fourteen days to Nuvem to shower all his love on her. Those fourteen most tragic, most important days of his life. That wasn't an impossible task because he loved her and love always resides in the moment and thereafter for Nuvem every moment was a realisation and expression of the fact that he really loved and cared for her. That was the best bargain God offered to him for taking away the best God bestowed upon him. And Nuvem's life was depleted forever.

But God's ways are great. God was not concerned whether Nuvem loved her or not because He knew Nuvem loved her the most in his life. All God wanted for Vrishti was she carried the conviction with her that she was loved by Nuvem as much as she had loved him. God tweaked her brain and granted Nuvem the power and way to express his love. Nuvem, and hopefully Vrishti believed he loved her both when she was conscious and unconscious during the time that was granted to them. And time had lost whatever meaning and value humans attach to it. Both were blessed in love – one in liberation, and the other in suffering.

Three things happened, Nuvem learned that caring for her was love because she cared for him all her life; his love reached her and she knew she was always loved which was true also; and she hopefully went happily to her heavenly abode.

But Nuvem was destined to carry the report card till he would live. There was no exoneration. There was no forgiveness. And he didn't want any for that might mean the end of love and death while he was alive. His love manifested his grief and made him humble and compassionate. Also, she had left him with a lot to ponder about – Did he deserve her? Whether he was a failure in his life, he didn't love her enough, and he deprived her of her due? She was the most beautiful woman in the universe, an even greater human, and completely adorable. Everyone loved her and she loved him. That was perhaps the mandate God gave her. She came into his life and blessed him, and when she went, she left him humble, compassionate, and much mellowed human.

Probably God's mandate also left him to ponder why didn't he show her the love he had for her. He realised that it was mainly because he wore the badge of his work as an achievement and pretentious authentication of self-praise, and self-importance. So, why did he overwork? He was a victim of wrong priorities which later became shackles of habits and he ended up feeling important and being defined by his work, but deprived of life. And his consciousness laughed aloud at the folly of his brilliance.

That was pure and sure stupidity for which he has paid through his life by neither accessing her love nor showering his love on her and would continue to pay a huge emotional cost of it for the rest of his life as well. And what a price to pay for a simple learning that love is happiness, and simplicity a blessing. Hopefully, he should remain centred till he lives and become a better human. That's the least he could do for her.

The creator of the universe has designed life in such a way that even with all-around success, He leaves the picture of life somewhere consciously incomplete. The presence of this imperfection is a constant reminder to stay grounded and be human.

His life too was incomplete and lost its sheen with her going away. As he thought so, he felt deep sorrow and tears once again swelled in his eyes. He felt sad that God had given him everything to live happily, and taken away the very basis of that happiness. Was hollow happiness sadness? The pain and helplessness in those tears were palpable but they made sense of love.

How strange is the justice of the creator? He keeps the picture of life incomplete to assert its paradox and value. And God shows the blessed that in this imperfection lies the essence of perfection ...! Implication – Instead of envying others' lives, we should thank the creator for the incomplete picture of our lives. Because our picture may not be as surgical as others' incomplete picture.

And then, Nuvem spoke to himself, "When something bothered me, I didn't talk about it with anyone. I thought about it all by myself, came to a conclusion, and took action that I felt suitable to the situation, alone. Not that I feel lonely, I think that's just the way things are. Human beings, in the final analysis, have to survive on their own, alone. The truth is so difficult to digest!"

By the time he got back from his emotional tour, it was time for lunch.

Baggage Drop Point of Life

"A man was driving on a windy road in the hills when his car toppled over while making a short turn. He tumbled out of his car as it fell into a deep gorge. Miraculously, on his way down, he managed to grab a branch of a tree.

The man called out to God with the greatest fervour. No reply came, and the tree was crumbling to the second. He did not give up and called out again a few times. A few minutes later a roaring voice broke out of the sky, "Let go of the branch," the heavenly voice said, "I will protect you." The man looked down and saw no chance of survival. He looked heavenwards and hollered, "Are you sure?" "Yes, let go," the voice said, "I am God." The man thought for a second and said, "Is there anyone else up there?"

Shibra woke up that morning at eleven and by the time she got ready after a hair wash, it was around twelve-thirty. The feeling of being home was sinking in and she was happy.

Shibra smiled, she remembered her Ammi scolding her for skipping meals, especially breakfast whenever she woke up late. After almost three years, Shibra opted to be scolded to get the feel of her home. She went straight to Zainab's room and before she could say anything, Shibra hugged her tightly. Zainab lovingly complained anyway because she had put in a lot of effort to prepare breakfast of her choice and even Nuvem didn't have breakfast.

Shibra immediately rushed to his room, got in without knocking, and before Nuvem could say anything she scolded him, "Why didn't you come for breakfast, Ammi had prepared South Indian today?"

"Because you did not wake up in time."

"Come on Senior, now that's not an excuse", she paused for a while, looked at his face, and said, "Hey, what's on your face dude? Where is your smile? Had a bout with your emotions, again? I thought you had managed yourself so well. I have been observing you since yesterday, you are not the same man I met at Fagu. Is Dehradun not suiting you?"

"You take a break, so many questions? I'm good, let's go for lunch.", was a much-measured response from Nuvem.

The dining table was well laid out and there was an air of exotic aroma in the dining room. It was some Peshawari Chicken dish he had never tried before. And, to say the least, it was delicious. Shibra was bubbling with the joy of coming home and chirping around in the glow of her Ammi's affection. Zainab was sober and balanced, and more relaxed with the presence of Nuvem.

For the sweet dish, it was mouthwatering mango panna cotta with Seviyan Kheer, (Vermicelli Pudding) which he really liked. Afternoon was turning more pleasant than he had expected and the warmth of a home away from home was reaching him once again. Women truly make a home.

It's funny. When you leave your home and wander really far, you always think you want to go home. But then you come home, and of course, it's not the same. You can't live with it; you can't live away from it. And it seems like from then on there's always be this yearning for some place that doesn't exist. After Vrishti, Nuvem was pushed into such a state, and he still yearns to discover that place. He is never completely home anywhere.

But after coming to Zainab's home, it felt like there was an unknown motivation to go back to his home in Jaipur. However, when he wanted to shift to his unit, both mother and daughter insisted he should stay for one more day. For Sunday, they had plans to show him their Rishikesh Resorts. Nuvem, somehow couldn't refuse and he agreed to stay with them for one more day.

It was quite embarrassing for him to repeatedly postpone going to his unit, but he couldn't do much about it. It was really strange he was enjoying the attention and affection of the family; he had just met a day before.

Zainab wanted to have coffee after lunch. Shibra politely excused herself and slipped into her room for an afternoon siesta. Nuvem was an ardent supporter of the afternoon nap and he would have any day taken that option, but for whatever reason, he agreed to have coffee with Zainab that afternoon.

Nuvem found it quite intriguing but he had to grudgingly give in to the fact that he was seeking Zainab's company. Everything happens for a reason, he met Shibra at a godforsaken place on a road bend at a higher altitude and in the most unlikely of circumstances, and now it seems the reason was perhaps finding a meaning in Zainab as well.

Nuvem was Vrishti's man. She will always be his priority and to that extent, he never felt an urge or need to seek any companionship. But there he was wanting to sit with Zainab. Life is a paradox indeed.

After Shibra went to her room, leaving them with each other, the initial few minutes were a personification of a silent awkwardness between them. Finally, Zainab broke the ice and asked, "You are missing Vrishti?"

Nuvem was not prepared for that question. He was caught off guard and he hurriedly said, "Why? No, I mean how do you know?"

Zainab knew that for sure and she confirmed the same in the nervous fumbling of his words and she replied, "Something triggered your feelings when we were having our morning tea in the garden."

"Yes, I was missing her." He didn't say that Vrishti's memory got triggered because of her striking resemblance with Vrishti and he remembered the quality times he had spent with Vrishti. Even Zainab knew she was the reason for by then she was aware of her striking resemblance with Vrishti. Nuvem wanted to wriggle out of the emerging situation where the focus was growing on him. He had to channel the conversation onto Zainab and so, he asked, "Even you were missing Salim Sahab, isn't it?"

"Of course, I miss him. But today my tears swelled up for your vulnerability."

"With the passage of time, I have managed my mind quite well. But Vrishti fills my thoughts most of the time and my emotions overflow sometimes. And strangely, every person or situation doesn't affect me. This only happens when I meet some people at random, both known and unknown, and I don't understand why I am not able to hold my feelings in front of them. I don't make much out of it but that's the way I think I honour her every time."

Zainab heard him patiently and thought maybe they met for a reason. There was definitely a bond, perhaps, of pain. She dismissed that stray feeling and said, "Let her go. It will bring a lot of peace to you. Please understand that Vrishti has gone, she is no more with you. Please honour her choice, maybe she didn't want to stay in this world anymore! And you accept and adapt to newer dynamics and vibrations surrounding you. You have to accept first and then adapt."

Love – A Dimension of God's Blessings

"The most painful thing is losing yourself in the process of loving someone too much, and forgetting that you are special too."

– Ernest Hemingway

Zainab was holding a lot in her heart. Shibra loved Salim and when they lost him, she was devastated. Unfortunately, she leaned on Shameer Sikander for emotional support instead of her mother and in doing so, she inadvertently hurt herself and Zainab badly. Shameer Sikander was a narcissist who didn't care about Shibra. He eventually betrayed her and broke her heart into pieces. That was a double dose of tragedy that struck and shook Shibra and pushed her into severe depression. One day, Shibra left home and Zainab was left all alone to bear the burden of her pain. There is an equanimity in pain, in the sense that it showers suffering fairly on everyone. But Shibra thought her pain was the greatest. She didn't want to involve Zainab for fear of hurting her but her decision to leave home eventually resulted in hurting her even more. And for similar reasons, Zainab didn't involve Noor. Although painful, that was perhaps a good decision. Noor had kids and family to take care of in the faraway US, she was a working woman as well, and the responsibilities of her home and office kept her busy. Noor had built her nest and she was happy. Zainab had no one to share her pain with and she silently suffered alone. It was her road and her road alone. Others could walk with her, but no one could walk it for her. In her case, no one even walked with her.

Nuvem was a sensitive man and he wore his emotions on his sleeves. He was manly enough to cry when he had to and took that strength to honour someone he loved and lost. His genuineness and honesty touched Zainab's tender heart and finally, she found someone with whom she could share her feelings without being judged. She didn't want to but she couldn't hold herself anymore. The accumulated feelings of her helplessness that lay buried in deep dark corners of her heart for a very long time found the flow and spilled out all over him.

She said, "In my case, the process of adapting began ten years ago and acceptance just kept on following. This is the case with every woman who loves her husband and children and her expectations of reciprocation are bellied every day and still she continues to give and love her family unconditionally. In her case, the process of adaptation always commences first and the acceptance follows closely as a natural consequence of her womanly prowess and survival instinct. But she pays a huge emotional cost for it and the cost is directly proportional to the time lag between the adaptation and acceptance. In our case, Shibra paid an additional emotional cost because she is beautiful, loving, more efficient, competent, capable, and daring in a world scripted by men.

And loving unconditionally is an innate strength of every woman. This is what makes her a woman of substance. Some women become frustrated and grumpy in the process, and a few of them get into a destructive mode and destroy their homes. But most women, after a particular age, compromise their happiness and right to receive love. They learn to preserve them in themselves, find peace, and live with it. Mind you, peace sits on a storm, and at times storm destroys her.

And the man she loves, more often than not, has to bear the responsibility for her sufferings. However, knowingly or unknowingly, this does not happen that way. And, some of the men are forced to accept their folly only after losing her. Such men need acceptance and adaptation to become more caring and compassionate while she is alive. Barring a few of them, the majority of men are brought up to behave manly, and they are denied the sacred emotional intelligence of caring for women in their lives. Men live in denial, and an unknown uneasiness a lot of time in their superficial lives."

What Zainab spoke, she spoke as a woman in love, and that made a lot of sense to Nuvem. Words may lose their sense in the perceptions of the listeners, but when feelings are spoken, words mean what they say. As Zainab spilled her long-suppressed feelings, her pain was visible in her eyes, though her face and tone were firm. It was like a crust formed over the molten lava of latent turmoil.

Nuvem tacitly accepted he was guilty of all the crimes of men she had recounted, yet he wanted his feelings validated through the mind and heart of a woman. And he said, "What you are saying may be true, but why should that happen?"

Zainab had touched his chords within and she knew it. She looked deeply into his eyes as if to gauge the sincerity of his quest. That was their first serious eye contact, and both became aware of the beginning of a vague but special bond building between them. What was that, human, or need for mutual dependence, or need to move on, or God's will?

But whatever that was, it was surreal. The eye contact broke when Zainab smiled, the smile that Nuvem interpreted as a statement of her knowing that he was guilty of what she said. He had to move on and that's why she talked about acceptance and adaption which are the strengths of a woman, even in reverse order.

But she also needed to dump some burden out of her head and feel lighter. And what better option than to do that before a stranger who will never be able to judge her? She said, "Our lives begin in love and thereafter follow the similar patterns and hues of relationships. These patterns which are harbingers of potential pain are mostly ignored and misunderstood by both men and women till it's too late.

This happens because our natures are different and that's a God-given, and what it leads to is weird and it is destiny. Destiny is a hiding place for the unknown. Most men don't intend to hurt a woman intentionally, but woman ends up getting hurt invariably. I feel most of the men are playful and there is a need for women to be a sport to tide over the problem.

But that's not to be, basic instincts play, men are molded by their ego, and women by love. This difference is the law of nature to balance and sustain the process of evolution. But that's not so simple. And the important question is whether that's unfair to women.

Ours was an intercaste love marriage. We both were graduates of IIM, Ahmedabad. My father was a school teacher in Delhi, Salim was from a family of bureaucrats, and his father was a very senior IAS officer of UP Cadre. This is their ancestral home where we live.

We both were working in New York. I was with KPMG, and he occupied the corner office of a renowned global investment equity firm. We met for the first time at a corporate get-together and slowly but steadily we built our lives together and eventually got married with the consent of our families.

The next five years were no less than bliss for both of us in New York City. I experienced love and that feeling of being in love, and being loved was beyond description. It was akin to experiencing divinity. I felt I was the most blessed woman in the world. Salim was a very sensitive lover who cared for me like his baby.

We were very attached to our India and our families, and thus we decided to wind up in the US and shift, lock-stock-and-barrel, to this home on the outskirts of Mussoorie. We had earned some good money and we mutually decided to invest the same in the business of tourism. That's how our three luxury resorts saw the sunshine, one in Naldehra, and two in Rishikesh.

The next two years since our return from New York were hectic but flourishing. We were on cloud nine of happiness as we welcomed our bundles of joy, Noor and Shibra into our blessed lives. Our love touched a new horizon and dimension in the blessings of God Almighty.

HOPE TRUMPS HURT

"I'm in love with the man you showed me in the beginning and I'm thankful for the memories we made. But I was forced to learn that in relationships, it's not about how they start, it's about what they continuously show. And I refuse to let the person you once were be the reason I let myself keep getting hurt by the person you have become."

Thereafter, the law of marriage caught up with us. Salim overworked for our business whose fame skyrocketed, and our love started sliding downhill. Our respective commitments, his business, and mine with our daughters, took him far from me.

We hardly spent time with each other, talked less, communication almost broke down, and intimacy between us diminished. The only sunshine between us was the presence of Noor and Shibra and that too for different reasons – He played with them, and I remained committed to bringing them up in the best possible manner.

Shibra was a bubbly child who grew very fond of Salim and she was far too young to be aware of the trauma of loss of love I was undergoing. Salim was a doting father who would pander to her every need, right or wrong, and I was the strict mother who always guided her on the honourable path a woman must take to be strong and independent in her life. I had no option but to see Shibra opt for love of a man which is only an illusion. A man is not meant to love, but a woman is nothing but an embodiment of love. Shibra was very talented but strong-headed. She was exactly the way I was as a young girl. Noor had a higher emotional quotient and she depended on me dedicatedly."

Nuvem was a loving man and he didn't go with what Zainab was saying about the love of a man. But she was emotional and he wanted her to go with the flow of her heart to let go of accumulated bitterness arising out of a felt but unfulfilled need of Salim's love. He wanted her to empty herself of the long unladen burden of expression of her internal discord. He did not judge her narration and allowed her to go on and unload her negativity without interruptions. It is always wise to let emotions win in their battle with logic.

Zainab had reached a stage where it did not matter who the listener was. The presence of Nuvem was no longer necessary because she got hooked on herself and in those exclusive moments, she didn't have to bother about what her words were conveying and to whom. In any case, words in certain scenarios, beyond obvious, don't necessarily have to have a meaning for everyone. In a Nimbus Cloud of Unknowing, where only SMOTH exists, words go beyond language and still make sense! SMOTH was Vrishti's word which has no meaning in any language and yet it was one word language that made sense to her when she was inching closer to her exit.

Zainab continued, "Not that Salim didn't love me but over time he had distanced himself from me and I felt deprived of the intimacy and support that I deserved from my life partner. I was treading on a lonely path. I was adapting myself to this new normal but acceptance was yet to dawn on me. I was hurt but hope was still alive. And one day I heard a hint of a rumoured extramarital fling of Salim Khan with a younger colleague at Naldehra which he never admitted and I never asked. That could be a construct of my imagination, but I never wanted to believe it. However, on that fateful day, my hope crumbled and I accepted that Salim had gone beyond the point of no return. It was one of the most difficult times of my life when Shibra was showing the early signs of depression and I was grappling with absurdities, uncertainties, and nasty mood swings of my menopause all by myself. But I sailed through those choppy waters because Shibra of late was understanding the woman in me and she was increasingly leaning on me for emotional support.

The process of acceptance was firming in. Maybe, love was never meant to be. Maybe, I had to live with that feeling, like a new skin that you never asked for. How do you accustom yourself to this new reality that's suddenly thrust upon you? After you have emotionally drained yourself, where does the strength to pick yourself up and continue come from? Because tomorrow will still come but it will be woefully mundane.

Take a holiday, perhaps, a solo one may be. I haven't done a solo one ever. The holiday sounded like the best idea of all days, nothing like a journey to find yourself. But what of the journey you've been taken off from?"

Zainab, typically, had been putting on a brave face, grinning-gritting in between the heaving breaths of chest waiting to explode. When a usually high-spirited and confident woman breaks into tears, in the full, cold glare of her questioning self, it perhaps humanises her even further. There is growing up, one that you've wished happened in private, but this catharsis in public – under an accompanying bar of Eurythmics, 'Sweet Dreams are Made of These' in the playlists of your heart – is cold, extreme, and open. It leaves you with no place to hide with a question, why was I so spent in such a good life?

With a small pause, she continued, "That feeling of being rejected as the woman who loved unconditionally became a rallying point for my womanly instincts and strengths to find me. That came from my disillusionment about everything but myself. I had no lure or desire for dresses or cosmetics or jewelry or sandals.

I decided to upgrade my loneliness to being alone. That moment was powerful and I told myself to stop being scared of doing things alone. Go to that café alone. Go shopping alone. Travel the world alone. You have to let go of the fear of being alone and stop being dependent on other people."

What she said hit Nuvem hard, especially the later part of her last sentence "Other people" and his thoughts got triggered. "Can our own become other people? Philosophically, yes, people other than yourself are others, however psychologically, my wife and my daughters, sisters, parents, and my friends are mine, they belong, and I owe that sacred belonging to them because I love them. But why am I having to bear that nasty feeling of being alone? Was Khalil Gibran right when he wrote, "Your children are not your children. They are the sons and daughters of life's longing for itself. They came through you but not from you and though they are with you yet they belong not to you." But I have to pretend not to believe him for I am living and I have to be a silent pillar of support to my daughters not only because they came through Vrishti but because I love Vrishti now through them and receive their love as a blessing of God Almighty. Similarly, Khalil Gibran also said some profound words of wisdom on marriage. He said, "Let there be spaces in your togetherness and let the winds of the heavens dance between you. Love one another, but make not a bond of love: let it rather be a moving sea between the shores of your souls." Nuvem knew Zainab was angry with herself, but strangely and rightly too she did seem to have clarity on what she was saying! Did Vrishti also think that way? Perhaps yes, and that answer made him feel uneasy. That which is not entirely true still holds some uncomfortable truths hidden in it. But the momentary transition of insights hugely improves perspective.

Nuvem spoke to himself, "Salim Khan and I have sailed in the same boat, unfortunately, irrespective of our truths. Salim had absolved himself of all his failings, if any, but I have to bear the burden while I am alive. Keep milling, keep smiling."

Unmindful of what Nuvem would think, Zainab continued, "My sincere efforts to find myself attracted the attention of both Salim and Shibra, and they took note of changes I was absorbing slowly, but surely. I had taken sure-footed steps towards myself – a quest that worked to ignite me in the innate strength of a woman who is forced to be in love with herself, and which every woman loves at some level or the other. It is a universal strength of every woman, even poor, rural, or uneducated, every woman.

So, what did I do? I became busy. I decided even not to rest during the day. It was an irony of sorts that Salim was comparatively free, and I created work to keep busy at home. Salim was an ardent fan of afternoon siestas, he needed one as a necessary necessity, the power nap that he thought energised him, and he would often ask me to lie next to him and steal some rest. But my deliberate and intentional aversion to resting during the day ensured an uninterrupted sleep of nine hours for me at night.

I knew I was closing the possibilities and avenues of our conversation. Yes, we did converse with each other only when we were with friends and relatives and that way, we were a much-loved couple in the environment. When alone, we would often keep quiet and fiddle with our mobile phones. I knew for sure Salim had taken me for granted, I was angry, and I became incommunicado to get back at him for ignoring me for so long. He had given me everything, but his love. And I didn't desire any other thing, but love.

I was surely submerging into myself. That was peaceful, I felt good, I felt stronger, I felt powerful, I felt unburdened, and most importantly, I felt happy."

At that juncture, their eyes locked once again with a hint of tears in them. And, ever so subtly, for just a fleeting second, Zainab smiled. It was a kind of smile you miss if you blinked – but that was enough to signal to Nuvem that she recognised the melody life played and that she still remembered it, and still thought of it to this day …

Zainab had just given vent to her feeling which probably remained unexpressed with the untimely demise of her husband. When Vrishti gave Nuvem the report card on his life, "You don't love me, you only love your friends.", he realised, she had totally misunderstood him and went on a tangent to internally tarnish and undermine his love for her. God was kind to give her access to his love in those last days of her life. But perhaps, she went unhappy because she loved him, cared for him, and didn't want to leave him alone after her. In fact, in her last moments when she felt she was being taken away, she spoke to our elder daughter, "Iska Mere Jaane Ke Baad Kya Hoga?" (How will he survive without me?)

Nuvem felt Zainab was unfair in her assessment of Salim Khan's love for her and she felt deprived of love by the misunderstanding that her love remained unrequited.

In their respective realities, the expectations of both the women were bellied by the very men whom they loved more than themselves. After all, how does a woman show her love, she cares, she supports, she understands the vulnerability of her man, she guides him, stands firm with him in times of his needs, and she meets and exceeds his expectations. That's how she shows her love.

And what does she expect in return, only a bit of his time, lively conversation beyond mundane, a bit of intimacy, and maybe, a word of appreciation for everything she does for the family, and that too selflessly? She works forever, even when she is not well. And she expects she be rewarded with some sensitivity, sincerity, and emotional enrichment.

Should insufficient reciprocation, albeit unknowingly by men, affect women to the extent that they deem it unrequited love? That's a little unfair, not true but real. But calling that a lack of love and suffering silently is a crime, a crime of perception. When a woman loves, she is a lover, and her man is beloved and the reverse is true as well.

Nuvem didn't want to go there, but Zainab ensured that he revisited the sacred corner of his thoughts.

Love is a Common Denomination

"When I kept you in the verses of my poetry, I didn't know that your name shall echo in every page I turn, over the chapters I intend to fill, blending with each word that dared to find space."

– busyreadin …

Zainab was emotional and she shared her pain with him. He respected her feelings and he even related to them. But perhaps Zainab may never understand that a man will only cry for one woman in his lifetime … after that, his soul will never allow him to fully fall in love again. Salim Khan loved her. Nuvem had that conviction because he loved Vrishti and she thought he loved his friends more than her.

There is always an inequality between a lover and beloved and the beloved is always at a disadvantage because her or his love for the lover is mostly undervalued by the lover. As Nuvem got thinking about the course correction that could have happened in the interpretation of his rights and wrongs, and after Zainab's literal confession of the pain of her love, he was not surprised by Vrishti's report card. He felt that love is always an individual experience of a woman and man in love. But it may never be a similar experience for them.

That may be because the hierarchy of their transient love was at a different level and the latitude of their happiness differed depending on interpretations within their inner realms. In Sufi traditions, often a beloved is only a stimulus for the stored-up love that had lain dormant within the heart of a lover for a long time hitherto.

And there is no method to understand who loves more or who loves less. Nuvem felt eventually it boils down to who experiences more and who experiences less. The roles of being a lover or beloved are not chosen; divinity assigns those roles to them. Poets have created and romanticised the pain of Majnu and Farad to highlight the concept of ishq through the sufferings of love, maybe for the right reasons, but in reality, perhaps, mostly women suffer in love. She is by nature a repository of love, but the reciprocal love of her man mostly falls short of her expectations, and she suffers. Even women who pretend not to care suffer such a syndrome of love.

It's not that their love is not acknowledged by men, but perhaps women being more sensitive by their innate nature are not able to access men's love for them in equal proportions. Perhaps, both Zainab and Vrishti loved their men more than themselves and the reciprocation by both Salim and him fell short of the expectations of their sheer sensitivity or even over-possessiveness. Over-possessiveness of love is a blessing too!

In Vrishti's case, she loved more and perhaps she felt that love was a solitary thing and feelings should always trump reality in the mayhem of emotions. That feeling, right or wrong, gradually pushed her into self-induced loneliness and consequent suffering only because she loved Nuvem from her soul. She was blessed by her love.

So, she housed her love within herself as best as she could and perhaps created a whole new world in her deeper realms – a world intense and strange, complete in itself. In fairness or unfairness, the quality and value of Nuvem's and her love were determined solely by Vrishti. And her sufferings too! She was a very good woman and goodness is expensive.

On a positive paradigm, however, love as a common denomination, presents an equanimity to its fairness. When we seek love, wisdom, and madness embrace each other in a tight hug. On the path of love, strangers become lovers and beloveds, and they are neither the masters nor the owners of their respective choices. We are only a brush in the hand of the Master Painter.

The path of love has many opponents – anxieties, avarice, fear, grief, greed, hate, lust, self-pity – all the usual friends. It's only if you dare to follow your heart that you may be happy in the journey of your love.

If we had the choice, most of us would rather choose to love rather than be loved. But unfortunately, our choices are chosen for us! Almost everyone wants to be a lover and the truth is that, in a deeper secret way, the state of being a beloved should be intolerable only because it causes misery to themselves and to those who love them truly. And that's an unfamiliar and unfair reality!

Nuvem knew he was trying to enter the domain of the unknown and manufacturing a reality and he had to stop. He also felt Sufi traditions of love are mired in tragedy and they focus only on a singular side of love. Love cannot be imprisoned in justifications because love is love either way and it cannot be measured by the human heart.

What happened has happened and it cannot be reversed and it should never become a reason for our pain and suffering post the demise of our loved ones. The guilt and grief are the residual negative emotions of the unexpressed love and thus they undermine the sincerity of human bonds. Nuvem had learnt that life and love are not mutually exclusive. If one honours life, he or she should honour the love they have for each other.

THE PERSISTENCE OF MEMORY

"I cannot speak, but I can listen. I cannot be seen, but I can be heard. So, as you stand upon a shore gazing at a beautiful sea, as you look upon a flower and admire its simplicity, remember me. Remember me in your heart; your thoughts, and your memories, of the times we loved, the time we cried, the time we fought, the time we laughed. For if you always think of me, I will never have gone."

– Excerpts from a poem by Margaret Mead

Thereafter, Vrishti was all over Nuvem's mind. Nuvem had healed himself to a level from where he could remember her with a smile. And with each passing year, the memories of their good times were outweighing those of his pain and suffering.

Sufficiently close to the point of losing her and immediately after her demise he encountered a psycho-emotional plunging region. His emotions plunged into it with such a massive force that his mind temporarily lost control over its sanity and balance That was the devil's home where the pain, grief, depression, and loneliness encaged him into an emotional servitude.

Nuvem realised he had made Vrishti central to the devil's home. She didn't deserve to be there at all. Vrishti is such a pure, pious, and beautiful woman who was languishing so long in that darkness for no valid reason. Zainab's outburst prompted Nuvem to ponder why should that happen.

And that happens because he doesn't lose Vrishti only once. He loses her hearing a song that reminds him of her smile. Passing a landmark. Laughing at a joke they would've laughed at. He loses her infinitely.

But she doesn't belong to darkness. So, he asks her, "Why can't you leave?" His voice breaks and an onslaught of tears blurs his vision.

And her response is prompt, "I have already let you go."

"But I didn't."

She pleaded, "I don't want to be a part of your plunging zone. I need to be a part of your happiness zone. That's the least I deserve."

"I understand that grief is love that has no place to go. Now my favourite thing about myself is being your husband. I know I share this grief with some, but no one else is your lover. Only me. And so, it's mine and the sadness will never go away. It'll always be with me."

"You remember always asking me why was I accelerating in a neutral gear? Now you are doing the same. I am not there. Who are you holding on to? We all have a chapter which we refuse to read out loud, something, that's bookmarked with the darkest shades we know, yet, goes unnoticed by people. A page that changed the whole course of our life, but we kept turning."

"I was always a happy man. Natural for me. You know it. And then you merged with eternity, I never trusted happiness since. I have never been the same since you were gone. There is a melancholy in me that never goes away.

I am 50 percent happy and 50 percent sad at any given moment and after losing you, I won't ever get out of it. Like that is I won't ever get over it and the more I know that and embrace it the better off I am.

I don't want to forget you and not even what it felt like when you were leaving. Because you deserve it.

That's how important you were to me!

So, if I have to suffer and if I have to be sad for the rest of my life and if I have to be lonely without you, I will be because of the particular thing, your sense of caring and giving and what you brought to my life.

That's the way I honour you."

"But I don't exist anymore. You can't hold on to nothing. You are only putting your happiness on hold. You need the closure. And closure is always logical for it paves a path for a beautiful life waiting to happen to you."

"There is no closure! Closure is an idea that many may believe in. But I have spent almost three years of my life waiting for closure, for a specific conversation to happen that I wasn't even willing to initiate in order to move on from feelings of pain and hurt. And I had to learn that if I am waiting for closure, probably I am not going to get it. Closure is this illusion that my pain belongs to someone else or you can come back.

And only to fix that, sometimes I hold on to illusions of letting go of what's real. I think closure might come from a place where I feel like I am not strong enough to let go on my own and I want to admit that letting go of you just hurts. And that feeling is okay. This is the power that I may have autonomy and authority over my life and that gives me the permission to heal and move forward and move on and let go."

"I don't agree with you because if you have autonomy or authority over your life you have to exercise that power to chase closure. Even after suffering for three years now, all you are doing is closing yourself off to that opportunity. The hard truth you have to learn is you are the only person who can give yourself happiness. And ironically, the only way to do that is by becoming more open. Open to all the new experiences, people, and love you can have in your life. Open, not in order to secretly get back at someone, but to be back to yourself."

"I don't want closure because I will continue to honour you because you left too early."

Vrishti was not convinced and she said, "You are as obstinate and crazy as ever. Sometimes heaven does not ordain a companion for us when we need them the most. Some of us are meant to travel alone. Our journey is not defined by coming together, but by letting go. Maybe, we need to love ourselves before we can love another or maybe, we are destined to live in hope. Either way, no feeling is final.

So, decide whether you want to honour me or make me happy though I have gone out beyond the idea of both honour and happiness. Since you feel me in you, please make that feeling feel happy.

Unless you revive your Awargi in your heart once again, you will remain plunged into a psychological darkness. Redemption begins as the plunging region diminishes with time and the mind is set free to find and authenticate the sense of sanity back into your life. Nothing is in your control, acceptance and surrender are automatic, and they are never complete.

Your decision to heal, as and when taken, hastens the process of acceptance and more importantly it will permit you the privilege of preserving me in the same form as you found me in your life.

Healing doesn't mean you'll never get triggered again, or that eventually you're going to arrive somewhere free of any pain or suffering. Healing is a quiet homecoming. It's about returning to yourself and settling peacefully into the truth of who you are. Not complete, broken but beautiful. Whole, lovable, human. This is Hiraeth in the true sense of your world.

You have to redeem yourself and you have to turn all your fears and concerns over to God and it will be an awesome journey thereafter. Though things will never fully return to normal after the loss of someone like me, the passing of time does begin to resemble normal. You had two choices, be bitter, or be better. I am sure you will choose the latter.

May you never go through that heartache again, and I am sure you won't. May God bless you beyond your expectations and land you at a stage when you can be grateful that you can grieve me and be able to celebrate me for the cherished life I had and the beautiful time we spent together.

And once you realise that, you learn to cherish what you have. You remember to hold the magic close, to embrace the fleeting moments that tell you, you belong, moments when you feel joy, when you know you are free, when you have daughters who see your need, and then, just like a shimmering firefly that flashes its light and disappears into darkness, you will have your one taste of heaven and it's worth a lifetime, every time.

And Zainab is a good woman …"

What is better – solitude or third-party companionship?? But Vrishti had decided to leave, leaving him with a poser why is the universal uniqueness of the man-woman relationship experienced by every man and woman individually?

Sonder

"People don't like love, they like that flittery flirty feeling. They don't love love – love is sacrificial, love is ferocious, it's not emotive. Our culture doesn't love love, it loves the idea of love. It wants the emotion without paying anything for it."

Both Zainab and Nuvem accessed the quintessential man-woman relationship with their respective perspectives. She thought Salim did not love her and Salim, having departed to heavenly abode, was not there to assuage Zainab's injured feelings and Nuvem could not allay his guilt because Vrishti was no more. None of them could defend anything against the law of nature and their opinions and perspectives only made their life more difficult. Surrender is the key that will open the avenues of acceptance and show them the only path available is to bury their grudges and celebrate their loved ones who have departed a little early.

So, who was wrong, one who could not express his love the way a woman wanted, or a woman who did not fathom the love of her man? After all, how love is manifested – through caring and sharing. Women are past masters of caring and sharing, and men by nature express their love by providence.

Unfortunately, after initial pampering, a woman is mostly not interested in the materialistic view of a man in caring for her, she craves his company. Women will never understand that a man loves only one woman in his life, he cries for her, and she remains his number one priority. He depends on her entirely and desires to be nurtured by her like a child. As opposed to that, after a while, a woman learns to be independent and as such she is always stronger in tackling the loss of a spouse better than a bereaved man.

Zainab must understand that her husband is the only person who has ever loved her for who she is. Her mom loves her because she is her daughter, her siblings love her because she is their sister, and Noor and Shibra love her because she is their mother. But her husband is on another level when it comes to loving her.

Nuvem didn't realise that his longish silence was a bit unnerving for Zainab who sat quietly observing changing hues of his facial expressions and even tears. She had no way of knowing that she pushed Nuvem to that silent zone with a heady cocktail of disagreement, guilt, understanding, misunderstanding, and perceptional challenges prompted by venting her stored-up emotions on him. And with due respect to her internal vanity, he broke that uneasy silence and said, "Maybe, you were a bit harsh in your assessment of Salim Sahab's commitment towards Shibra and you."

It was difficult for Nuvem to say that because he considered himself guilty of not loving Vrishti enough. He had to measure his words before he spoke and yet maintain the flow when the whole process was against the grain of his nature and they hardly knew each other. There was another reason for his apprehension and that was because his daughter had only allowed him to judge others. He was not supposed to pronounce the judgement on anyone.

Surprising, Zainab nodded her head in agreement and said, "You are probably or maybe you are right. And this realisation struck me when the idea of a solo trip was conceived in my mind. Contrary to my expectations of a usual cold response, my decision of going on a solo trip raked up a storm in the tea cup of my family."

The teacup reminded him of the need for a good cup of tea. Unlike Vrishti and Zainab and like Salim Khan, Nuvem's afternoon siesta was a sacred ritual for him to keep him psychologically active. And as soon as that urge for tea knocked his mind, he saw tea and some crisp cookies being brought by one of their helps and he could no longer hold his happiness.

The happiness was of an unstated need being met and he felt Vrishti smiling on him from above and saying, "For a blink of a second your thought strayed towards me," she gave a broad smile which was ever beautiful. He smiled too.

Zainab saw that bright smile on his face and she too smiled, and said, "Salim always said, smile, while you smile, there will be miles and miles of smile, only because you smile. This tea for both of us is in reverence to you sacrificing your sacred siesta for me today."

Finding the similarity between Zainab's story in his story, Nuvem temporarily strayed into a sonder – a profound feeling of knowing and unknowing that each random passerby lives a life as vivid and complex as theirs. Each populated with their own ambitions, friends, routines, worries, and inherent craziness – an epic story that continues invisibly around them like an anthill sprawling deep underground, with elaborate passageways to thousands of other lives that both of them will never know existed, in which each one of them might have appeared only once, as an extra sipping coffee in the background, as a blur of traffic passing on the high way, as a lighted window at dusk. And that's the larger truth.

Philosophically, sonder is a kind of collective loneliness of the people passing randomly around us, but appropriately it's also a loneliness of unknowing. The same was the case with Zainab and him. They came to this world alone and they were incapable of knowing the feelings of people around them. Leave aside others, they weren't even aware of their own feelings, most of the time. For a blink of a moment, Nuvem realised his inability to read the minds of others was indeed a blessing.

After that refreshing cup of tea and his quick touch with Sonder, Zainab said, "The idea of my solo trip was conceived in my mind when I suspected Salim's infidelity. Salim and Shibra vehemently opposed my solo trip because they didn't want to let me go all alone and thereafter, they became overtly protective of me. Both Shibra and Salim offered to accompany me on a family trip. Unfortunately, they failed to gauge the build-up of my emotional turmoil that led to my decision to do a solo trip. They were not entirely wrong because despite whatever I thought, perhaps, they loved me and cared for me.

That was a gnossienne moment of realisation for me - A moment of awareness that people we've known for years still have a private and mysterious inner life, and somewhere in the hallways of their personality is a door locked from inside, a stairway leading to a wing of the house that they've never explored – an unfinished attic that will remain maddeningly unknowable to them because neither of them has a map, a master key, or any way of knowing exactly where they stand. That's how the life is. Everything we think may not be correct because we often judge and go by our judgements which many times are nothing more than the figment of our imaginations. So, don't believe everything we think!

This awareness also leads to unknowing because a lot of life is lived alone in our heads, and the noises and silence of the world cannot often cover the chemistry and physics of many of those feelings. It's an irony of unknowing that draws us apart from those who are destined to be our own in our lives.

We have our moments and the moments contain eternity. The idea of a solo trip reignited the sleeping vibes of the family.

When the glow of affection of Salim and Shibra reflected on me, I shelved my intended solo venture. Salim started caring for me. Perhaps he always cared for me, however, after I decided on a solo trip, he began to show that he always cared. I believed him and I was happy.

However, like everything else in life, our happiness ended when Salim died.

When Salim died everything in my life was forever altered. My nervous system changed. My capacity for life changed. My perspective and what I valued as important shifted. People left my life and others entered. The boundaries I needed to set were different. What I valued changed. Who I valued changed. What I could tolerate changed. My personality changed. My mothering changed. My purpose and passions changed. What I thought about life, death, and why we are on this Earth changed. At times it feels like I'm orienting myself to a life that's new and foreign to me, in a world where sometimes I still feel like a stranger and quite lost."

And just as the shades of pain began to show signs on Zainab's face once again, Shibra walked in and the moods lightened up.

FEAR – WHO CARES

"I think some of us were just meant to experience life more deeply. We don't just feel the breeze but we hear the earth speaking to us. When others cry, we cry too. We're painstakingly present, yet can feel the past and future existing simultaneously. We're highly aware of the beauty and pain of the world and long for a future where the good that's been lost can be restored."

The next day when they met over the morning tea, Zainab commenced from where she left the previous day. "I had a very personal connection with the idea of women running away from the traditional setups to find their own purpose, fulfill their own desires, and have their own adventures. But when Shibra fled from herself and left home after Salim's demise, it was the most heartbroken moment for me. I was anxious, I was worried, and I was hopeful. I prayed she be safe and return home after complete healing. Thank you for bringing her back.

I suppose my decision to go for a solo trip was to take off in the end, it was very much open-ended because life could throw any kind of curveballs at me, but the idea that I was on my own in this adventure and making all decisions was empowering. For me, that was always a lovely way to end a conflict agitating within me because the future holds so much possibility.

I am a mountain woman. I was born in the mountains and lived a major part of my life in them. Mountain is a strict father. It teaches us to be strong. But I was eying the silence of the depth. I was never an ocean woman but the expanse and depths of oceans always fascinated me. I somehow felt I would find peace on a beach. I just wanted to sit by the ocean for a while and watch waves coming in, forget everything, and just breathe.

My solo trip began as a Yoga vacation and I attended two weeks of mightily restorative Yoga classes at Agatti Island. I had decided to extend my stay since I was already all the way over there in Lakshadweep and I learnt Yoga as a prelude to my agenda of inner peace. What I wanted to do, actually, was to find someplace very remote to give myself a ten-day retreat of absolute solitude and absolute silence.

So, I shifted to a smaller and quieter Kadmat Island. Kadmat, an island in Lakshadweep, is located between Amini Island in the South and Chetlat Island in the North at a distance of some four hundred km from Kochi. There is an airport on nearby Agatti Island, in which flights operate from Kochi. From Agatti, it is two and half-hour boat ride to Kadmat. Ferry services also operate from Kochi on the coast of Kerala but involve a journey of sixteen hours. In Kadmat coral growths and multicoloured coral fishes abound in its lagoon area. Kadmat is one of the most important places in the world to me.

When I look back at the year that elapsed since my husband went away and Shibra slipped into depression after her relationship with Shameer Sikander fell apart, I see a detailed chronicle of total pain. And the moment when I came to this tiny island all by myself was the very worst of that entire dark journey. The bottom of the pain and in the middle of it. My unhappy mind was a battlefield of conflicted demons. There were noises, loud noises of uneasiness surrounding me from every direction and I felt I was floating in a very small boat without oars and I was being thrown and tossed around in violent waters of my inner depth. I had to steady my boat by my own resolve and live with honour, all alone. I guess life is all about doing it yourself, DIY …

As I made my decision to spend ten days alone and in silence in the middle of exactly nowhere, I told all my warring and confused parts the same thing, "We're all here together now, guys, all alone, let's survive, or else everybody is going to die together, sooner or later."

This may sound firm and confident, but I must admit this, as well – that sailing over to that quiet island all alone, I was never more terrified in my life. I hadn't even brought any books to read, nothing to distract me. Just me and my mind, about to face each other on an empty field. I remembered that my legs were visibly shaking with fear. Then I quoted to myself one of my favourite lines ever from my mom, "Fear – who cares?" and I disembarked alone.

I rented myself a little hut on the beach for some rupees a day and I shut my mouth and vowed never to open it again until something inside me had changed. Kadmat Island was my ultimate truth and reconciliation hearing. I had chosen the right place to do this – that much was clear. The island itself is tiny, pristine, sandy, blue water, and palm trees. It's in the shape of a teardrop and you can walk the whole length in over an hour. Tears are tiny in a vast ocean, and yet they exist as an ocean of emotions we carry within. Kadmat is located near the equator, and so there's a changelessness about its daily cycles. The sun comes up on one side of the island at about 6:30 AM and goes down on the other side at around 6:30 PM, every day of the year. The place is inhabited by Muslim fishermen and their families. There is no spot on this island from which you cannot hear the ocean. It is one of the quietest places I've ever been. The sounds of the ocean are an embodiment of silence.

Every morning, I walked the length of the island at sunrise and walked again at sunset. The reflective silence after a mindful walk brought peace …. The rest of the time, I just sat and watched my emotions, watched the fishermen. The Yogic sages say that all the pain of a human life is caused by words, and silence contains all the joy. We create words to define our experience and those words bring attendant emotions that jerk us around like dogs on a leash. We get seduced by our own mantras (I'm a failure … I'm lonely … I'm a failure … I'm lonely …) and we become monuments of them. To stop talking for a while, then, is to attempt to strip away the power of words, to stop choking ourselves with words, to liberate ourselves from our suffocating mantras.

It took me a while to drop into true silence. Even after I'd stopped talking, I found that I was still humming with language. My organs and muscles of speech – brain, throat, chest, back of the neck – vibrated with the residual effects of talking long after I'd stopped making sounds. My head shimmied in a reverb of words, the way an indoor swimming pool seems to echo interminably with sounds and shouts, even after the kindergartners have left for the day. It took a surprisingly long time for all this pulsation of speech to fall away, for the whirling noises to settle. Maybe it took about three days.

Then everything started coming up. In that state of silence, there was room now for everything hateful, everything fearful, to run across my empty mind. I felt like a junkie in detox, convulsing with the poison of what emerged. I cried a lot. It was difficult and it was terrifying, but this much I knew – I never did want to be there, and never wished that anyone was there with me. I knew that I needed to do that and that I needed to do it alone.

The only other tourists on the island were a handful of couples having romantic vacations. Kadmat is far too pretty and far too remote a place for anyone but a crazy person to come visit solo. I watched these couples and felt some envy for their romances, but knew, "This was not your time for companionship, Zainab. You have a different task here."

An Enigma That is Silence

"It is difficult to live alone, but when you learn the art of being alone, you find yourself. Then you don't need companionship. You realise you only belong to yourself. And yet you crave a third-party company ..."

I wanted to hear the sound of silence. The sound of silence seems to be an oxymoron. But when you are alone, in a reasonably secluded place, away from the hustle and bustle, stop to listen to the solitude. You will find that it has its own voice, its own music, and its own story. You only need to have the time and patience to listen. It's only that you have to tune in to the wavelength of emptiness.

Surrender yourself to the inner symphony and feel positivity and happiness take over gently but surely so that you are meandering along a path of cheerful musings. Some would say that this is a form of willful self-hypnosis. And they would be correct in large measure. But, to them, I would say, is there anything wrong with wanting to be happy? In fact, wanting to be happy should be a prime objective in life!

Yet others will call it the voice of your soul that you hear in communion with the Absolute, of which it is a part. And they too would be correct. For, when you give free rein to your spirit to roam freely in the heights and depths of the unknown, you fathom the possibilities that you need to strive for. The universe is permeated with a presence of benevolence, waiting to be discovered.

The consequence of this effort is self-awareness. This is the reason why seekers throughout the ages have been known to observe Maun Vrat (abstinence from speech) from time to time, to stop speaking and begin to listen to their inner selves; listen to the sound of silence. That is because it is only when you listen that you learn.

So, I kept away from everyone. People on the island left me alone. I think I trough off a spooky vibe. I had not been well all year. You can't lose that much sleep and that much weight and cry so hard for so long without starting to look like a psychotic. So, nobody talked to me.

That's not true. One person talked to me, every day. She was someone within me. My friend within who I recognised. She was myself. And this known and yet unknown she was on to me. Nobody asked me who I was, and nobody else bothered me, but this relentless someone would come and sit next to me on the beach at some point every day and demand, "Why don't you ever talk? Why are you strange like this? Don't pretend you can't hear me – I know you can hear me. Why are you always alone? Why can't you ever go swimming? What's wrong with you? "Who has tied you up? Why can't you break free?"

I was like, back off, whosoever you may be! What are you – a transcript of my most evil thoughts?

Every day I would try to smile at her kindly and send her away with a polite gesture, but she wouldn't quit until she got a rise out of me. And inevitably, she always got a rise out of me.

She ran away laughing. Every day, after she had gotten me to respond, she would always run away laughing.

I'd end up laughing, too, once she was out of sight.

I dreaded this pesky me and looked forward to her in equal measure. She was my only comedic break during really a rough ride. Saint Anthony once wrote about having gone into the desert on a silent retreat and being assaulted by all manner of visions – devils, and angels, both. He said, that in his solitude, he sometimes encountered devils who looked like angels, and other times he found angels who looked like devils. When asked how he could tell the difference, the saint said you can only tell which is which by the way you feel after the creature has left your company. If you are appalled, he said, then it was a devil who had visited you' If you feel lightened, it was an angel.

I think I know what that little punk was, who always got a laugh out of me.

On the ninth day of silence, I went into meditation one evening on the beach as the sun was going down and I didn't stand up again until after midnight. I remembered thinking, "This is it, Zainab." I said to my mind, "This is your chance. Show me everything that is causing you sorrow. Let me see all of it. Don't hold anything back."

One by one, the thoughts and memories of sadness raised their hands and stood up to identify themselves. I looked at each thought, at each unit of sorrow, and I acknowledged its existence and felt (without trying to protect myself from it) its horrible pain. And then I would tell that sorrow, "It's OK. I love you. I accept you. Come into my heart now. It's over." I would actually feel the sorrow (as if it were a living thing) enter my heart (as if it were an actual room). Then I would say, "Next." And the next bit of grief would surface. I would regard it, experience it, bless it, and invite it into my heart, too. I did this with every sorrowful thought I'd ever had – reaching back into years of memory – until nothing was left.

Then I said to my mind, "Show me your anger now." One by one, my life's every incident of anger rose and made itself known. Every injustice, every betrayal, every loss, every rage. I saw them all, one by one, and acknowledged their existence. I felt each piece of anger completely as if it were happening for the first time, and then I would say, "Come into my heart now. You can rest there. It's safe now. It's over. I love you." This went on for hours, and I swung between these mighty poles of opposite feelings – experiencing the anger thoroughly for one bone-rattling moment, and then experiencing a total coolness, as the anger entered my heart as if through a door, laid itself down, curled up against its brothers and gave up fighting.

Then came the most difficult part, "Show me your shame," I asked my mind. Dear God, the horrors that I saw then. A pitiful parade of all my feelings, my lies, my selfishness, jealousy, and arrogance. I didn't blink from any of it, though. "Show me your worst," I said. When I tried to invite these units of shame into my heart, they each hesitated at the door saying, "No – you don't want me in there … don't you know what I did?" and I would say, "I do want you. Even you. I do. Even you are welcome here. It's OK. You are forgiven. You are part of me. You can rest now. It's over."

When all this was finished, I was empty. Nothing was fighting in my mind anymore. I looked into my heart, at my own goodness, and I saw its capacity. I saw that my heart was not even nearly full, not even after having taken in and tended to all those calamitous urchins of sorrow and anger and shame; my heart could easily have received and forgiven even more. Its love is infinite.

I knew then that this is how God loves us all and receives us all, and that there is no such thing in this universe as hell, except maybe in our own terrified minds. Because if even one broken and limited human being could experience even one such episode of absolute forgiveness and acceptance of her own self, then imagine – just imagine! – what God, in all His eternal compassion, can forgive and accept.

I also knew somehow that this respite of peace would be temporary. I knew that I was not yet finished for good, that my anger, my sadness, and my shame would creep back eventually, escaping my heart, and occupying my head once more. I knew that I would have to keep dealing with these thoughts again and again until I slowly and determinedly changed my whole life. And that this would be difficult and exhausting to do. But my heart said to my mind in the dark silence of that beach, "I love you; I will never leave you; I will always take care of you." That promise floated up out of my heart and I caught it in my mouth and held it there, tasting it as I left the beach and walked back to the little shack where I was staying. I opened an empty note page of my mobile phone – and only then did I open my mouth and speak those words into the air, letting them free. I let those words break my silence and then I allowed my thumbs to document their colossal statement on the page:

"I love you; I will never leave you; I will always take care of you."

Those were the first words I ever wrote on that note page of mine after coming to Lakshadweep Islands and which I would carry with me in my mind from that moment forth, turning back to it many times over the next two years, always asking for help – and always finding it, even when I was most deadly sad or afraid. And that note page of my mind, steeped through with that promise of love, was quite simply the only reason I survived the next years of my life.

Whenever I see an unapologetic woman doing her own thing without trying to be likeable, my first thought is: can you please sit down with me and tell me how you managed to unlearn years of conditioning and achieve this state of mind? Is there a cheat sheet that you can share?

And surprisingly the Self responds, "Unless you learn to face your own chaos, you will continue to stay unconscious to the magnitude of your own light."

The Island of Kadmat taught me the process of accepting and adapting which guided me on a path of letting go and lighten up.

Let Go and Lighten Up

"Leave the old you and your old ways behind and look forward with the new you. A butterfly doesn't return to its former self or choose a life of crawling and cocoons once it has met the sky. It has wings now. It has been transformed. Set free. Someone once said, "You can't talk butterfly language to caterpillar people." It simply won't be understood. You have an entirely new flight language and an entirely new flight path, and your whole body, mind, and spirit will naturally flow."

– Butterfly by Ullie-Kaye

And that path for me passed through the process of "Adapt and Accept." I always adapted and then accepted. But after Kadmat, I learnt to accept things first and then adapt. I didn't even bother if there was any difference as long as it didn't interfere with my happiness. The art of acceptance gives us the ability to remain calm and flow with life. It helps us to travel light, as it frees us from the extra baggage of expectations, anxieties, and anticipations. We learn to accommodate people and situations rather than resist them or judge them as right or wrong. We also do not hold them responsible for our emotions.

Acceptance also carries shades of appreciation, motivation, love, and respect. As we experience and practice acceptance, we experience greater acceptance from others.

Acceptance does not mean everything is perfect. It only means that our state of mind is perfect. Acceptance does mean to let things be the way they are. It means keeping our minds stable and working on the situation. Acceptance of what has happened is the first step to start working toward the solution. We need to accept our own self along with our mistakes or difficult Sanskar first, and only then we can focus on corrections. Acceptance allows us to be free from the shackles of denial and move forward creating a new path. Accepting other people means we accept that they are different from us – our mind does not get disturbed, it remains detached from their Sanskar.

The art of accepting situations means we understand this is it, rather than question what is this and get into why, where, when, and how. As we accept the situation, our mind becomes silent and stable. Our efficiency and decision-making powers rise. Kadmat taught me that to shift our focus from the problem to the solution, four prerequisites are highly helpful for adapting to our acceptance.

Firstly, when we need to change – a habit, lifestyle, job, house, city, social circle, or make changes in our thoughts, emotions, and attitude, we need to recognise how open are we to the change. In a world of rapid changes in people and events, adaptability is not only an important quality but also a very essential ability that we need to possess at all times. Adaptability is the companion and operational component of acceptance.

Secondly, when there is change around us, there needs to be a change within us – an inner preparation before outer adaption.

Thirdly, instead of sticking to old comfort zones created by past experiences or past beliefs, be flexible. We have the power to adapt to any person, any situation, any place, any job, and any environment. Within a few days, this change will also become our comfort zone.

Lastly, practice meditation, and interpersonal communion with inner self and Supreme daily, to increase our power to accept, accommodate, and tolerate. Since adapting is a matter and process of breaking the old and rigid thought patterns, remember and remind yourself that we are always one thought and one decision away from adapting and flowing with life.

Facing negative emotions such as pain, hurt, guilt, and grief is a universal experience that tests our emotional resilience and inner strength. These emotions often arise from situations over which we have no control and it is natural for us to be consumed by bitterness and negativity as we delve into the insensitivities of life. This often leads us into a cycle of rumination and resentment, trapping us in emotional turmoil.

One of the most empowering realisations in such moments is recognising that we can choose how we respond to these emotions. While we cannot control much, we can take responsibility for our own emotions and reactions. And for that, we have to go through our own Kadmat(s). Each one of us.

It's a crucial step towards reclaiming our inner peace and happiness. Central to this is the practice of letting go. Letting go doesn't mean pretending that pain doesn't exist. Instead, it is a conscious decision to release ourselves from the grip of bitterness and resentment. It is about freeing our own hearts and minds from the burden of our guilt and grief. That way letting go is an act of self-liberation and it lets us create space for healing and growth within ourselves.

By acknowledging reality and maintaining control over our own feelings and reactions, we empower ourselves to navigate through our rough patches and tough times without losing the sense of our inner peace and integrity.

Therefore, the courageous choice lies in letting go of disappointment, unpleasantness, and compulsions of adamant rigidity. This doesn't mean memories will be erased, but it is adorning them with a pleasant outlook and positive reflections.

This involves accepting what has happened, learning from it, and consciously deciding to focus on positive growth and healing. It is a process that may take time and effort, but it is a journey worth undertaking for our well-being.

As we release the hurtful emotions that bind us, we create space for gratitude, compassion, and resilience to flourish within. It is a challenging but transformative experience. In letting go, we reclaim our power. We move forward with a lighter heart and clearer mind, ready to embrace a brighter and more fulfilling future.

Letting go is not a sign of weakness but a testament to our strength and resilience in adversity. It's a courageous step toward personal liberation and emotional freedom. This is moving forward with a lighter heart and a free spirit. That's the way to honour our loved ones who have left. I say this because our loved ones have to be happy wherever they are. The universe is interconnected and every vibration, positive or negative, happy or sad, will reach them. You have no choice but to be happy and happiness is the imperative of our inner discipline.

Companionship Beyond Relationship

"Out beyond the ideas of wrongdoing and right-doing, there is a field. I will meet you there. When the soul lies down in that grass the world is too full to talk about."

– Jalal-ud-Din Rumi

After a refreshing experience over an extended weekend in Dehradun, a sense of hiraeth set in and Nuvem wanted to go home. He felt longing for his home once again and he accepted Vrishti would never be there. Now he wanted to take care of Vrishti's home. On his way home, he visited his unit. He had to visit his Paltan because Paltan is always a Maiti Ghar (Maternal home) for a Gorkha Soldier.

Time moves slowly, but it flies. Nuvem's solitude was firming in and he knew in the end he only had himself. Slowly and surely, he was arriving at the "Zero Expectation Zone" of his life. That was a serene phase where his expectations started deserting him and surprisingly that was a regretless self-empowerment.

Vrishti remained embedded in him and gave him company at her pleasure. She could walk in at will and mingle smiles to his tears. He didn't want to part with her precious company, but time was taking her further away from him. He felt the pull, but she too was slowly becoming a distant memory. He hated time for that. Having lived without her for almost five years, and having been adrift in life for all those years, he was organising him in a relationship with himself.

Nuvem was aging happily. Some of his childhood buddies had exited the departure lounge and taken their flights to permanence. A lot was changing, but his daughters loved him more and Nuvem had learnt not to be central to their charmed lives. That was the main reason for his happy aging or so he believed.

But time is a function of divinity and it had to eventually land Nuvem into the warmth of destiny where Vrishti would finally become his imagination. It was only two years since he returned from Dehradun and five years after she died.

Shibra was doing well and she regularly kept in touch with him. Sometimes, Zainab called too. But she constantly intruded on some of his thoughts. He liked her but did not want to take that forward.

Meanwhile, in Dehradun, Zainab was searching for a new universe around her. A universe where Shibra would surely be settled like Noor, but along with them she wanted Nuvem in it as well. Zainab was perfectly happy in her boring life before Nuvem came to her home. She was languid and killing time, like a character from some sad story. That indolence stopped when Nuvem was introduced to her by Shibra. Shibra trusted Nuvem and she had encouraged and prodded Zainab to once again open up to life with him. But that won't happen without her desire to move on ... No begging, no pleading just an honourable flow of life.

That decision to move on was made easier by Nuvem because he was a caregiver by nature, and she could picture him going in a kind of orbit around her, making her the key directional setting for his compass, and growing into the role of being her attendant knight. She felt Nuvem was a kind of man who desperately needed a woman in his life – but not so that he could be taken care of; only so that he had someone to care for, someone to consecrate himself to. It would be lovely to be treated that way. It also scared her because she wondered if she was capable of being somebody's sun, somebody's everything. Was she centred enough now to be the centre of somebody's life?

But somehow, she never dared to bring up the topic with Nuvem for she was not sure if she was confident enough to broach the subject. She had not even searched his heart, all she knew, he might not be thinking that way about her. She liked Nuvem. It was none of his concern, of course, what she felt… He is an Army man who has managed to live alone for a long time without getting too entwined in somebody's life and societal expectations.

Zainab sometimes went far in her quest for life with Nuvem. She questioned herself and answered them herself at her convenience. So, what will become of me and Nuvem? Now that there is, it seems a "me and Nuvem?" She often imagined being told by Nuvem, "Sometimes I wish you were a lost little girl and I could scoop you up and say, "Come on live with me now, let me take care of you forever." And she would tell herself, "But you aren't a little lost girl. You're a strong woman of substance with a career, with ambition. You are a perfect snail: you carry your home on your back. You should hold on to that freedom for as long as possible. But all I'm saying is this, don't burden your life anymore, and cherish your newfound clarity and charisma."

She often spoke to herself a lot – "I'm not sure what I want. I do know that there's part of me that has always wanted to hear a man say, "Let me take care of you forever," even though I have heard it spoken before. Over the last few years, I'd given up looking up to that person and learnt how to say this heartening sentence to myself, especially in times of fear. But to hear it from someone who is speaking sincerely …"

One day, on his birthday, as Nuvem lit a single candle on a single pastry to celebrate his singlehood, Zainab landed up at his home in Jaipur with a single rose, a red rose to wish him on his birthday. His black-and-white world suddenly turned multi-coloured.

And there was no awkwardness between them. She gave him a big hug. It was warm and passionate and that contained the give and scent of a woman. That one minute of intimacy surpassed the logic and Dastoor (Rituals) of the world.

And that teleported them into a new universe, a universe that was in a realm where they stargazed while they lay together on the drops of due spread over the green grass of pure joy. That was the zone where being intimate with someone wasn't about being physical with someone. Intimacy didn't come from a place of physicality. It's about trusting someone because they make you feel safe. It's about sharing your deepest fears, insecurities, and vulnerabilities with someone who embraces you for who you are without judgement. It's about being able to open up about your inner thoughts, your pain, your past, and your trauma to another person, knowing that they will listen with empathy and understanding.

Zainab had two tickets for Agatti Island.

When the captain asked the cabin crew to prepare the cabin for landing at Agatti, Zainab suddenly grew apprehensive of uncertainty and the happiness of a newer life before taking the final plunge into the unknown yet again. She went with the flow of her thoughts from the heart. She was coming back to Kadmat Island under notably different circumstances. Since she was last there, she'd circled the world, settled their family business, survived the going away of her husband, erased all mood-altering medications from her system, learnt to speak a new language, sat upon God's palm for a few unforgettable moments in Kedarnath Dham. She was happy, healthy, and balanced. And yes, she could not help but notice that she was sailing to this pretty little tropical island with a man other than Salim. Which is – She admitted it! – an almost ludicrously fairy-tale ending to this story, like the page out of some housewife's dream. Perhaps even a page out of her own dream, from years ago. Yet what kept her from dissolving right now into a complete fairy-tale shimmer is that solid truth, a truth which was veritably built in her bones over the last few years – She was not rescued by a prince; She was the administrator of her own rescue.

Her thoughts turned to something she read once, something that Zen Buddhists believe. They say that an oak tree is brought into creation by the two forces at the same time. Obviously, there is the acorn from which it all begins, the seed that holds all the promise and potential, which grows into the tree. Everybody can see that. But only a few can recognise that there is another force operating here as well – the future tree itself, which wants so badly to exist that it pulls the acorn into being, drawing the seedling forth with longing out of the void, guiding the evolution from nothingness to maturity. In this respect, says the Zen, it is the oak tree that creates the very acorn from which it was born.

She thought about the woman she had become lately, about the life she was living, and about how much she always wanted to be this person and live this life, liberated from the farce of pretending to be anyone other than herself. She thought of everything she endured before getting there and wondered if it was her – She meant, this happy and balanced her, who was now dozing on the deck of this fishing boat – who pulled the other, younger, more confused, and more struggling her forward during all those hard years. The younger Zainab was the acorn full of potential, but it was the older Zainab, the already-existent oak who was saying the whole time; "Yes – Grow! Change! Evolve! Come and meet me here, where I already exist in wholeness and maturity! I need you to grow into me!" And maybe it was this present and fully actualised Zainab who was hovering over sobbing her five years ago, and maybe it was this her who whispered lovingly into her ears that everything would be okay, that everything would eventually bring them together here. Right here, right to this moment. Where she was always waiting in peace and contentment, always waiting for her to arrive and join her. The ocean has been swaying her, the sun shining.

The little fishing boat anchored right off the shore of Kadmat. There were no docks on that island. They had to roll up their pants, jump off the boat, and wade in through the surf on their own power. There's absolutely no way to do that without getting soaking wet or even banged up on the coral, but it was worth all the trouble because the beach there was so beautiful, so special. So, she and her Nuvem took off their shoes, they piled up their small bags of belongings on the top of their heads and they leapt over the edge of that boat together, into the sea. And said, "Let's cross over …"

There is an exquisite feeling many of us had as children, that everything is good, that every day promised more excitement and adventure, and that nothing could ever thwart our joy for the magic of it all. But somehow as we grew into adults, responsibilities, problems, and difficulties took their toll on us, we became disillusioned, and the magic we once believed in as children faded and disappeared. It's one of the reasons why as adults we love to be around children, so that we can experience that feeling we once had, even if it's just for a moment.

Zainab and Nuvem felt that the magic they once believed in was true, and it was the disillusioned adult perspective of life that was false. The magic of life was real – and it was as real as they were. In fact, life could be far more wondrous than they ever thought it was as children, and more breathtaking, awe-inspiring, and exciting than anything they had seen before. When you know what to do to bring forth the magic, you will live the life of your dreams. Then, you would wonder how you ever could have given up in believing in the magic of life!

Maybe Zainab and Nuvem were not getting across how fun was all that. Truly, it was so much odd and satisfying fun, trying to figure all that out. Or maybe they were just enjoying this surreal moment in their lives so much because they happened to be falling in love, and that always made the world seem delightful, no matter how insane was their reality. Zainab would often think about all such beautiful things every morning at sunrise when nature splattered beautiful colours in the sky to see that stray cloud become so meaningful. (Nuvem too means cloud in Brazilian Portuguese)

Nuvem thought he was sorted. And sorted he was because, with both Vrishti and Zainab, he realised that a woman is a shade better than friends. She is a companion beyond looks and relationship. He often contemplated and rethought his different status in life. He would very often tell Zainab, "Look, I'm seventy years old. Believe me, now I don't want to know how the world works. I recognise that you don't love me yet the way I love you, but the truth is that I don't really care. For some reason, I feel the same way about Vrishti and our daughters that I feel about Shibra and you – that it wasn't your job to love me, it was my job to love you. You can decide to feel however you want to, but I love you and I will always love you. Even if we never see each other again, you already brought me back to life, and that's a lot. And of course, I'd like to share the rest of my life with you. Let's celebrate our loved ones because who we are now is because of Salim and Vrishti and our daughters."

And when the replacement from God arrives, you will forget what you have lost. Was Zainab a replacement sent by God? But can anyone replace Vrishti in Nuvem's heart even if Zainab is God sent? Sure, God is an authentic idea but God's love is irreplaceable and loss irreparable and irreversible. Is reality truth or truth reality? Is there truth in fiction? You may not see reindeer fly, but you will see the things you've always wanted …

Their companionship was unique. When asked about them, they would simply say: that they were two souls, loving each other quietly. Not lovers caught up in passion, nor friends with shared memories. In the city's chaos, they found comfort in their unique bond – where understanding flowed with words, and empathy blossomed in silence. They weren't a couple, nor were they friends; just two people connected in a way that's hard to explain.

Zainab and Nuvem accessed their respective happiness once again on the music of the time.

Dance Freely with Wound Beneath Your Feet

"Even on the darkest of nights, when the world goes quieter, and you feel all alone, you will still feel the pounding of your heart beating in your chest, the friendly reminder that you are a living breathing human being and you are never truly alone."

– veronicarosewriting

Zainab was a compassionate woman. She scripted renewed insights into their togetherness and got Nuvem back to almost what he was when his Vrishti was alive. With her caring ways, he learnt to dance again with a wound beneath his feet. He learnt that victimhood was a kind of cruelty to himself. He understood that a life lived with happiness and positivity could not be remembered only with grief. A definitive chronology of hard-earned insights infused a lot more life into their lives and blessed them with their respective share of well-deserved happiness.

Nuvem lost his wife Vrishti on September 05, 2021. As she breathed her last, he stood numb by her ICU bedside. Their daughters, Mish and Niu were holding her hand infused with IV fluids. It was sudden, most unexpected. Over the days that followed, there were prayers, and visits from many who shared their experiences and love.

Finally, it was over. The condolences and the mourning. Only the grief stayed. Every simple routine activity brought back memories. Nuvem decided months afterwards that he would resume his routine and take charge of his life. But it's the hardest thing to do.

Especially when he lived 39 years with a woman who had so many facets. A brilliant mind, compassionate, passionate, and so caring and giving. She worked in a school and enjoyed teaching children.

Vrishti built her stature over time. She did not pursue philanthropy as an act of charity. She loved giving every moment of her life. Even beyond the wallet. Despite such extensive and intensive involvements, their daughters and he never felt unloved. She was always there to share little experiences through the day. Birthdays, anniversaries, achievements of the family, everything was celebrated. Vrishti genuinely believed in family values. She had great admiration for successful women across professions. And she carried this sensitivity to her home as well. She wanted Nuvem to be himself, and evolve in his own unique way, and she encouraged and enabled him to be the person he is today – confident and independent. She would smilingly introduce herself as "Nuvem's Vrishti."

Their daughters were at the core of her being. Her love never overwhelmed or pressured, it was quiet but strong steering them to be good humans compassionately.

Vrishti's warm demeanor was the way she viewed the world – with happiness and positivity.

Nuvem has befriended his mourning for his wife. But he doesn't want to remember her with grief and negativity. Else, she will frown from the heavens above. Yes, there is deep pain, but this is one loss that can be soothed with the celebration of her life.

Nuvem accepted mourning can be a sign of well-being and hope. Everything and everyone we love, we eventually lose. Imagining this inevitability pragmatically can make mourning a source of meaning when it's done right.

Being remembered and honoured is the only residue left behind by a worthwhile life. Mourning is a special kind of missing humans do. Our imaginations get busy, and we look back and wonder who the person was, what the relationship was, and what it all meant. We judge, we daydream, and look for signs and symbols. Mourning grounds us in here and now, even as we recast the loved one in imagination and memory. It is a healing process, as this past is woven into the present that continues. It's like the oak and acorn story.

Mourning, Sigmund Freud wrote, "is a manifestation of human health, the good counterpart to the pathological condition of melancholia. This is because mourning ends, and we get back to ordinary life. Humans have the capacity to love and to be attached, and this transforms mere change into loss. To love is to love something vulnerable, and make ourselves vulnerable – should they die, we do not move on, we suffer their loss. Unlike change, which is impersonal and keeps happening, transience implies loss and wistfulness. Transience and mourning arise together."

Mourning can be a sign of a well-lived life. Having said that we need to explore the idea of repetition, much discussed in psychology, the mind's tendency to loop back over and over again over traumatic events in the same fated patterns. But it is possible to cast that repetitive process as helpful rather than neurotic. It is a kind of repair work, an imaginative alchemy that accommodates the loss to live on. Mourning is a transition, where morality and blame are suspended.

Of course, some situations simply go beyond our mind's capacity to absorb and work out. But if we do survive these adversities, we emerge from mourning transformed by painful loss and active imagination.

This casual exploration of the mechanism of mourning must lead us to our innate strengths which are noble, beautiful, and fine because they allow us to delve into the unknown inner realm and make us generous and wondrous. This open spirit can move and change those who witness it and this is what makes mourning an affirmation of life, rather than a state of bitter degradation.

This opening of the heart has its origins in the infantile state, when we are suckling at our mother's breast. It is the beginning of gratitude when we are on the receiving end of a loving gift, where nothing is demanded in return. In acknowledging that one has received goodness, one welcomes goodness. This cycle of repetition builds confidence. Those who experience this psychological attunement realise that we, others, and the world itself, are unearned gifts.

Gratitude is an acknowledgement of this fact, and it is the essence of what allows hearts to open up towards each other. So, even as we mourn, we remain thankful for what we had, and the world that we passed through.

Nuvem always knew that happiness is not a cliché. Life is beautiful. Life is the most precious gift of God. Life is a treasure of jewels whose worth is immeasurable. Life shows all its colours and shades which may be dark and bright. The dark shades of life make us realise the depth of life because life is just not a bed of roses. As it is rightly said, "The stream would have no song if it wouldn't have rocks in its beds." So, the trying, enduring episodes of life make us more insightful and patient. They make us view life from a different perspective, and help us explore new possibilities. The pain and suffering in life make us judge the importance of the pleasure that is the beauty of life.

There is no dead end as such there is no shortcut in life. What may seem like adversity is actually an opportunity. Failures are the stepping stones to success and success is counted the sweetest by those who never succeed.

When we are confronted with the idea of giving up at a point in time, that helpless situation perhaps opens new doors for us as life is full of surprises and possibilities. When we are shattered and lose courage, God helps us to pray and by praying we become humbler and tolerant in life. The more we pray the more optimistic and vibrant we become in life. Then we see the colourful shades of life, the joy, the ecstasy, the rhythm, the humour, the love. It makes us rejoice and celebrate. Celebrate not just because we have won a lottery, got a promotion, or planned a destination wedding. Celebrate just because we have made all the lovely things around us happen, the smile we give to our friends, the kind words we say to the people around us.

That is the beauty of life to see the sunshine which brightens our day and fills us with new vigour and strength. Each day is a new day to accomplish new tasks and usher in a new vision. Embrace the moment with tenderness and innocence and life will become a garden of mesmerising flowers.

Life is to pick up the good and ignore the bad. When we reflect on the positive aspects of life, we can cherish our dreams. Life is not a competition or a game of win or lose but it is an enjoyable journey, and we are a comfortable traveller as we always land safely.

Life is to forget and forgive. Move ahead with faith and conviction then only we can realise our dreams. Life will truly unfold its magic and bring good luck and happiness.

So, live life wholeheartedly as this day is yours and tomorrow may be more wonderful.

LET US NOT POSTPONE LIFE

"Not everyone you want in your life wants you in theirs. So don't burn yourself out trying to look good or do them favours when they really don't care if you're there or not. Focus your energy on those who truly appreciate your presence and appreciate you for who you are. Life is too short to invest time and effort in people who are not right for you. Surround yourself with those who make you feel valued and who support you every step of the way."

– Robert De Niro

We humans tend to think we come into existence when we are born. We imagine we possess our cells and atoms – but we are just borrowing these, from the food we eat, and the air we breathe. These atoms are ours for the tiniest moment. If we trace the energy that goes into our thinking, our heart beating, our blood pumping, we'll see this has always existed. Eventually, the atoms in your fingertips and brain, the carbon in your body, go into the centre of the stars. Astronomy is very humbling – it teaches us that we are the products of so many things happening in the universe. Looking back at these galaxies helps us learn how the universe began to put life together, starting with the earliest stars, with the complex materials that formed other stars, and eventually – in one galaxy, around one planet – we formed. All these things had to happen and go right for us to be here – this teaches us life is incredibly precious. We, humans, don't treasure life in the way we should or see it as this magnificent product of 14 billion years of things happening. We tend to look at trees, plants, and other animals and think we can do what we want with them because we are better than them – but they are just different expressions of the same idea in the universe, which is putting all life together, atom by atom.

All of us converge from wherever upon the blue planet, our spirits ignited by the promise of Life's grandeur. Years of silent battles will be a pilgrimage into the depth of self, a quest for resilience, and an unyielding will.

People who were strangers at the beginning will become companions. This tapestry of humanity, woven on the fields of play, will be a testament to the interconnectedness of the human spirit, a reminder that we are all part of a larger whole. We will learn the art of rising from the ashes in the crucible of competition. These moments of adversities will serve as catalysts for personal growth.

On the playfield of life, the journey itself is the greatest reward. The playing field, whether physical or metaphorical, is a sacred space for the soul to unfold. As the saying goes, "The journey of a thousand miles begins with a single step." Every game, every play, every moment is a step towards self-mastery – the value of the process over the outcome.

The spiritual perspective of people will underscore that the true essence of life lies in the journey only. Whether we stand on the podium or not, we will leave the quest enriched by the profound spiritual lessons we learnt, carrying forward a deeper understanding of ourselves. "The only real failure in life is not to be true to the best one knows," the Buddha said.

Eat like you love yourself. Move like you value yourself. Speak like you respect yourself. Live like you care for yourself.

Life will not postpone our death. So, let us not postpone our life.

Happiness

"Think of the life you have lived until now as over and, as a dead man, see what's left as a bonus and live it according to Nature. Love the hand that fate deals you and play it as your own, for what could be more fitting?"

– Marcus Aurelius, Meditations, 7.56–57

Nuvem felt he was having a course correction. He was working for a long time to switch to happiness and get back to his true nature. While sitting on the balcony of their Mussoorie home at sunrise he often contemplated happiness, his Kadmat Nirvana.

Life is a probability and as such living is a daring adventure. Moments are the measures of our life. Moments don't belong to us; we belong to moments. Moments accept our ownership of them only once before they leave us and leave us with another. The divine play is an outcome of the natural impulses of consciousness to express the totality of its self-knowledge in the movement of time, an impulse arising out of our quest for living. None of us are getting out of here alive. So, let's stop treating ourselves as an afterthought. Eat delicious food. Walk in the sunshine. Jump in the ocean. Say the truth that we're carrying in our hearts like a hidden treasure. Be silly. Be kind. Be weird. There's no time for anything else. The joys of life come from encounters with new experiences, and hence there is no greater joy than to have an endlessly changing horizon, for each new day to have a new and different sun. If we want to get more out of life, we must lose our inclination for monotonous security and adopt a helter-skelter style of life that will at first appear crazy. But once we become accustomed to such a life, we will see its full meaning and incredible beauty. Recognise the futility of accumulations, prefer minimalism, and invest richly in experiencing. This is beautifully summed up in two Latin words – Dum Spiro, Spero: While I breathe, I hope; and Dum Vivimus, Vivamus: while we are alive, let's live.

I must ask myself: Have I lived a happy and fulfilling life? And I answer: Yes, sometimes! And if I can be happy some of the time, I will probably lead a fulfilling life the rest of the time! As babies in arms, we do a lot of crying. Then there's that first laugh, the sweetest sound in the world – a baby's chuckle as he or she discovers a funny world awaiting exploration.

We'll need that laughter for the rest of our lives. It's a gift, especially if we can learn to laugh at ourselves as well as at the crazy world outside. A cheerful disposition has seen me through difficult times. It is doing so even now, as I wander the world, both internal and external.

Happiness will come my way if I don't run after it. Chase a butterfly and it will fly away. Stay still, and it may settle on my hand. And if I can summon up the laughter in my soul, I'll be fine, a friend of mine.

We can't be happy all the time, but we can certainly be happy some of the time. And here are some of the ways in which we can discover the joy of being alive.

A new day is the greatest gift of all – a new day, a new beginning, a new phase of life spanning out before us. Don't miss out on the miracle of each dawn. Be up with the lark or the rooster, open your window, or step out on your balcony and watch the sunrise in all its glory. The horizon is bright red, then orange, then apricot. The dawn wind greets us. The early morning light spreads over the mountains, over rooftops, over the fields and forests, and oceans. Then the sun takes over. Here it comes, spreading its golden beams over your home, over the land, over the planet – giving life to the earth, to plants, trees, birds, beasts, people! Without that sun, there would be no life on the planet. Greet it, salute it, for it signals a new day, a new beginning.

Simplicity is a pleasure … And mind you it takes a lot of discipline to be happy. But happiness is always simple. The early morning cup of tea. (As long as I don't have to get up to make it.) The rising winter sun slanting through the window and spreading across my bed. Sensual delight as it caresses me. A hot buttered toast for breakfast and don't forget two boiled eggs. Pen in hand, I sit down to write. The white, lined writing pad looks beautiful. Must I deface it? Just a few words and sentences. The afternoon siesta. On a cold, rainy day, it lasts until evening.

In the late December, sitting around the heater with family, and missing Vrishti. In late January, sitting around the stove with family and missing Vrishti. Sipping whiskey nice and slow and laughing away to glory and still missing Vrishti. Missing Vrishti is happiness, a routine, and discipline.

Savour the moment with Zainab, and make it count. Soak up the sunshine; and if it's cloudy, admire the cloud patterns; if it rains, take a deep breath and take in the cool clean air, the scent of the earth – for it too must breathe.

Read a little, write a little. Listen to music. Take a long walk. And if walking is difficult, go for a drive with her. And if you can't do that, open the window and look at the birds, the trees, the cats, dogs, mules, and monkeys … look at the people, no two of them are the same.

Will we see them again? Will we come this way again? Who knows?

We must learn to laugh, laugh at ourselves, laugh at life. People who don't laugh are seldom happy. Don't laugh at others. Seek out your own inconsistencies and laugh at yourself. A sense of humour gives you just the right balance in your journey through life.

Laugh at the ducks in the pond. Laugh at Sabita cleaning our home. Laugh at Devender in the branches of our pomegranate tree. Laugh at Brahma Bhai cleaning our cars. Laugh at that tiny bird splashing about in the bird bath. Laugh at the nest she stitched in a flowerpot. So fragile and so safe. Laugh at the sum that's giving you so much trouble in math class. Better than crying over it. Look at yourself in the mirror and have a good laugh.

And one must dance and dream too. Dance in the middle of the road one night. When asked, "Why are you dancing on the road," Say, "Because I am happy." And when asked, "And why are you so happy?" Just say, "Because I am dancing on the road!" Trust you are in love with yourself.

And so, I asked myself: Do I dance because I am happy, or does dancing make me happy? Do I sing because I am happy, or does singing make me happy? Do I write because I am happy, or does writing make me happy? I am never quite sure.

Above all, hold on to your dreams. If you have a dream, pursue it, hang on to it, and don't let it slip away when times are bad. A dream will sustain you, keep you going, give you a destination, something to live for. And if you hold on to it long enough, you might find that it leads to many good things.

I love you Vrishti … I will try to be happy come what may.

www.ingramcontent.com/pod-product-compliance
Lightning Source LLC
LaVergne TN
LVHW041201150826
845673LV00001B/247

* 9 7 9 8 8 9 6 9 9 5 1 0 4 *